THE SECRET OF THE
SILVER DOLPHIN

A newscast announcing a reward to anyone who can locate a valuable silver dolphin involves Louise and Jean Dana in a baffling search. Judy Platt is desperately trying to find the silver dolphin mentioned in her dead brother's will. But no one knows what kind of dolphin to look for—a live mammal or a silver object.

The Danas' sleuthing is hindered by a hostile fortune-teller and an elusive thief. The two are engaged in a sinister conspiracy to get the reward—and will stop at nothing to ensure the success of their criminal scheme.

Louise and Jean's quest for the silver dolphin leads them to Miami, Florida, and then to a deserted Caribbean island. A dangerous skin-diving chase, followed by an amazing undersea discovery, results in the Danas solving this intriguing mystery.

"I hereby put an unlucky sign on you girls,"
the woman intoned

The *Dana Girls* Mystery Series

THE SECRET
of the
SILVER DOLPHIN
By Carolyn Keene

GROSSET & DUNLAP
A National General Company
Publishers   *New York*

PRINTED IN THE UNITED STATES OF AMERICA

CONTENTS

THE SECRET
OF THE
SILVER DOLPHIN

CHAPTER I

Missing Inheritance

"—Most peculiar case. A reward is being offered to anyone who can find the silver dolphin."

Louise and Jean Dana stopped short in the doorway of their Uncle Ned's "cabin," as he called his study at home, to hear more of the radio newscast. But it ended.

Captain Dana, skipper of the transatlantic ship *Balaska*, winked at his nieces, who were home from boarding school for the Christmas holidays.

"Now's your chance to solve a mystery, my hearties," he said.

The girls' eyes gleamed in anticipation. "What's the rest of the story?" asked seventeen-year-old Louise, who had dark hair and soft brown eyes.

Jean added, "What is the silver dolphin? I want to start looking for it."

Uncle Ned chuckled at the enthusiasm of his

blond, impulsive niece who was a year younger than Louise.

"And claim the reward, eh?" he teased. "I know very little about the case, but my friend Hampton Howell can give you all the facts. He's head of the trust department at our Oak Falls National Bank, and has been settling the affairs of a widower who used to live here. The man came back just a month ago and died soon afterward. Everything checked out satisfactorily except one item in the will—a silver dolphin. Mr. Howell and others have searched everywhere but haven't found it."

"Does anybody know what the silver dolphin is?" Louise asked.

"Apparently not," her uncle replied.

"Let's go see Mr. Howell," Jean urged. "There's plenty of time before lunch and I've finished all my chores."

Captain Dana said he was too busy to go. "I must take advantage of every minute while my ship's in dry dock. But I'll phone Hampton for an appointment for you girls." He picked up the telephone on his desk and dialed the number.

While he was talking to the banker, the girls whispered to each other.

"Do you suppose the silver dolphin is a live creature?" Jean speculated.

"In any case," said Louise, "it must be valuable, or it wouldn't have been mentioned in the will."

By this time Uncle Ned had finished talking to

his friend. "You girls can go right over and see him. Mr. Howell's private office is in the building next to the bank. I wish you luck."

Louise and Jean thanked him and hurried off. They paused to tell their Aunt Harriet, the captain's sister, where they were going. The bachelor brother and his unmarried sister had inherited the old Dana home. Louise and Jean, who were orphans, had lived there ever since they were small children. They adored Aunt Harriet, who was sweet and motherly, and Uncle Ned, who was jolly, but when the need arose, a strict disciplinarian.

The girls decided to walk to the business district of Oak Falls. There was little traffic until they reached the center of town. They were surprised to see a great crowd of people in front of the office building where they were heading.

"There must have been an accident," Louise remarked as the sisters drew closer. "Oh, my goodness! Look at that man—climbing up to the second story!"

The man was pulling himself up by a rope he had thrown through a hook for holding a flagpole and had nearly reached a window marked:

HAMPTON HOWELL
TRUST DEPARTMENT

"Come down here!" a woman screamed. "You can't beat us that way!"

The crowd was violently pushing their way into the lobby, where a guard was hopelessly trying to stop them. Over the heads of the mob, Louise and Jean could see some of the people jammed together in front of the elevator, while others were leaping up the stairway.

"What's going on?" Louise asked a man next to her as the girls joined the throng on the sidewalk.

"You mean you're not one of them?" he answered in amazement. "Then you'd better get out of here before you're crushed to death."

The words were barely out of his mouth when a big red-faced man elbowed his way past Jean, knocking her off balance. As she fell against a woman next to her, Jean realized she had stepped hard on the stranger's foot. The woman cried out in pain.

"I'm sorry," said Jean. "Terribly sorry."

At that moment two policemen forced their way into the crowd. "What's your business here?" one of them shouted.

"To see Mr. Howell," most of the mob answered.

The Danas were thunderstruck. Why would so many people want to see him? Then the thought struck them—was it because of the broadcast? Were these people reward seekers?

The policeman called out sternly, "Do any of you have an appointment?"

"You'd better get out of here!" the man warned

"No, but I'm going to see him anyway and no-body can stop me!" one man cried belligerently.

The Danas were pushed to the curbstone, but Jean cried out above the protests of the onlookers, "We girls have an appointment with Mr. Howell."

At once all eyes turned on them. The policeman called, "Let them through!"

The unsympathetic mob paid no attention to the command. Louise was being squeezed so tightly her breath was coming in gasps. "M-maybe w-we should come back l-later," she whispered to her sister.

"No sir," said Jean. "Let's rush the crowd!"

By this time the policeman had made his way to the girls. "Follow me," he directed.

Finally they reached the elevator in safety. Due to the disturbance it had not been running. The officer, who had been joined by his fellow police-man, now called into the shaft, "Okay, Joe! This is Officer Reilly. Bring the car up." He turned to the girls. "Joe phoned us from the basement and we told him to stay there."

In a few seconds the elevator arrived. As the po-licemen barred the way to others, the Danas slipped into the car and the door slammed shut. When they reached the second floor, several people were mill-ing about in frustration and complaining because Mr. Howell's door was locked.

Just as the girls reached it, a middle-aged woman

came out. Her dark-complexioned face was red, and her black eyes looked like two smoldering coals below a mass of black hair. She was muttering something in a foreign tongue.

A young man, presumably Mr. Howell's assistant, who was holding the door asked quickly, "Are you the Dana girls?" When they nodded, he said, "Come in!"

Louise and Jean squeezed through the narrow opening just ahead of an onrushing group and again the door was locked. The girls were ushered from the waiting room into an attractively furnished front office. A man of about sixty, gray-haired and handsome but somewhat haggard looking, arose to greet the girls.

"I'm glad to see you," he said, "but forgive me if I seem upset. That broadcast, which was repeated several times, has made my life miserable the past two hours. We had no idea the response would be this great and were not prepared for it. I've been besieged by people who are sure they can find the silver dolphin."

"There are a lot more people in the lobby," Jean said, smiling.

"Well, they aren't getting in here," the trust officer said firmly. "One man even tried to come in the office window, but I told him to climb down the same way he got up."

"We'd like to hear more of the silver dolphin story," said Louise.

"Of course. And I hope you girls can solve this baffling mystery and receive the reward." Mr. Howell smiled at his callers. "I understand you're very good detectives."

"Just amateurs," Louise answered, but in her own mind she was recalling the exciting adventures she and her sister had experienced in their two latest cases, *Mystery of the Stone Tiger* and *The Riddle of the Frozen Fountain.*

Mr. Howell said that the deceased man, Oliver Platt, forty, who had no children, had moved to the Royal Oaks Motel outside town only a month before. He had gone to a lawyer to have a will drawn and named the bank executor of the estate. "Mr. Platt said he had brought all his cash and securities to this bank, and always carried his checkbook and safe-deposit-box keys with him. He told the lawyer he was not well."

Louise asked in surprise, "Did he leave the silver dolphin to someone?"

"Yes, his sister. Everything worked out according to his instructions—the relatives who were to share in the estate have been found. But there was nothing for the sister—she's not much older than you Danas—except the mysterious silver dolphin."

Jean spoke up. "The broadcast suggested you had looked everywhere for it. May I ask what kind of dolphin you were looking for?"

"Oh, a piece of jewelry or an art object."

"Couldn't Mr. Platt's family give you any clues?" Louise asked.

"Not one. It seems that Mr. Platt was a very quiet, uncommunicative person, and his family sometimes didn't hear from him for months at a time."

"What business was he in?" Jean questioned.

"Platt was a scientist. He had done some teaching in general science in a high school but gave it up and apparently lived on money he had inherited."

"Then he probably traveled extensively," Louise guessed.

"Yes," Mr. Howell agreed. "The family thinks the silver dolphin is some art object he brought from a foreign country. But where he kept it is the big riddle."

Louise asked, "Didn't anyone question Mr. Platt about the dolphin?"

The banker smiled. "His lawyer, like many attorneys, never became inquisitive in dealing with his client. However, Mr. Platt said he would tell him at another time what the dolphin was. But he never had a chance. The poor man was found dead in his room the next day."

"How tragic!" said Louise. After a few moments' pause, she asked, "May I see a sample of Mr. Platt's handwriting and any papers he left? There may be a clue in one of them."

Mr. Howell opened the safe in his office and took

out Mr. Platt's notes which the lawyer had left with the trust officer. Louise and Jean read them carefully, but there was not a single clue to help them find the silver dolphin.

But presently Jean said, "Here's something unusual." She pointed to the signature on one sheet.

Above the name were three stars arranged in a semicircle, and a lone star below it.

The trust officer nodded. "Mr. Platt signed his will the same way, but no one has any idea what the significance of the stars is."

"I'll bet," said Jean, "if we could find that out, we could solve the mystery!"

Louise agreed and asked if the girls might have a copy of the starry signature. Mr. Howell assented and quickly had his secretary make a photostat. As soon as it was ready the Danas said good-by, promising to work hard on the mystery.

The waiting crowd had diminished somewhat and the police were trying to coax the rest to leave. Louise and Jean hurried home. As they approached the front stoop of the Dana house, the sisters noticed that a woman was following them.

"Louise, she's the one who came out of Mr. Howell's office in such a rage!"

"She still doesn't look very pleasant," Louise remarked.

The stranger hurried toward the girls. In a heavy Spanish accent she said, "I am here to make a bargain with you. I think I know where the silver dolphin is. Meester Howell will not give me the reward for what I see in my crystal ball. For my information you will give me half the reward, yes?"

At once the Danas were on their guard. If Mr. Howell had not been interested, this woman must be a phony.

"Sorry," said Louise, "but my sister and I would rather work alone."

The girls started for the door. They were astonished when the woman barred their way, her eyes blazing and her fist upraised. "You cannot refuse Maria Castone! I get what I want! You work with me or you will be in great danger!"

CHAPTER II

The Fortune-teller

THE door of the Dana house was flung open and Uncle Ned came striding out. "What's going on here?" he demanded.

Maria Castone stopped harassing the girls and glared at him defiantly. She did not answer his question, however.

Captain Dana turned to his nieces. "I said, 'What's going on here?'"

"This woman, who says her name is Maria Castone, has been threatening us," Louise replied.

"Threatening you? Why?" Uncle Ned frowned.

Louise told what had happened. The woman had started to hurry off, but all three Danas followed her down the walk. "I want an explanation of this!" the captain ordered.

"I'll tell you nothing," Maria replied. She raised

her arms and began moving her hands back and forth in crisscross fashion. "I hereby put an unlucky sign on you two girls!" she intoned.

"Better make it good," Jean remarked with a laugh. "We don't believe in signs."

Maria Castone's eyes flashed fire. "You will not laugh when bad luck comes to you," she said. "And it will come soon."

Uncle Ned moved ahead and stood in front of her. "Where do you live?" he asked.

"I will not tell you," the woman answered in a sullen tone. "But you will not have to look for me. I will be back!"

She pushed past Captain Dana and strode off swiftly down the street. Louise and Jean and their uncle stared after her, puzzled. Finally the captain said, "I guess you're right, Jean. That woman is queer in her top story. Well, my hearties, don't think any more about her. Let's go inside."

Louise, uneasy about the woman, said, "You know I'm not superstitious, but Maria Castone worries me. She was acting queer down at Mr. Howell's office and now she has threatened us because of the reward for finding the silver dolphin. I'd like to find out where she's heading."

Captain Dana patted his niece on the shoulder. "Sound thinking. I'll get the car and we'll follow her."

He brought the sedan to the front of the house. Meanwhile, Jean had run inside to tell Aunt Harriet where they were going. Then she and her sister hopped into the car and the three drove off. Uncle Ned kept a little distance behind Maria Castone, who seemed to be unaware she was being followed. She did not turn around once, but hurried along at a fast pace. Finally the woman turned into a section of town where many Spanish-speaking people lived. Presently the Danas saw her go into a small shop. They slowly drove past.

"Well, for goodness' sake!" Jean burst out. "What do you know about that?"

On the shopwindow, which was fully curtained, was a neatly printed sign:

MARIA CASTONE
FORTUNE-TELLING

"Humph!" said the captain. "That explains everything. She's a fake."

"If she is, she may be a dangerous one," Louise said. "Uncle Ned, how about your going in to have your fortune told, so you can size up both Maria and her place?"

"Me? No siree!" Captain Dana said firmly. "After our little set-to at the house, I'm sure she'd be hostile. Furthermore, I'll tell you right now, I don't believe in fortune-telling. It's true that certain people are born with extrasensory perception, but as for predicting the future, I think it's a humbug. More people have gotten into trouble by listening to some phony palmist than there are one-dollar bills in our local bank. My advice to you girls is to stay away from here." He laughed. "Unless, of course, you're going on detective business."

Jean said quickly, "Uncle Ned, that's just the point. We certainly do have business with Maria Castone. First, to find out why she has cast an unlucky spell on us, and second, why she is trying to get information out of us and collect part of the reward."

The sea captain looked admiringly at his niece. "I might have known I couldn't get the better of you in a debate about sleuthing. Okay. But I still think it would be unwise to have Maria tell my fortune. Let someone else go whom she hasn't met."

"How about Aunt Harriet?" Louise suggested.

"Good idea. We'll go home and ask her."

At first Aunt Harriet was a bit reluctant to take on the assignment, but finally she consented. Uncle Ned and the girls dropped her at the corner of the street, where they would wait. Miss Dana sauntered down to the fortune-teller's studio and went inside.

Half an hour later Aunt Harriet returned, smiling, to her family. She stepped into the car and sat down beside Captain Dana. "I got my money's worth," she announced. "I believe you have figured this Maria Castone all wrong. She is really good. Why, she told me I had taken long trips. You know I have. Also, she predicted that somebody who works for me is going to have an accident. You know Cora, she's always getting into trouble."

Cora Appel, the Danas' part-time maid, was away on a few days' vacation.

"What else did Maria tell you about the future?" Louise asked.

Aunt Harriet grinned. "She said some of my family were going on a long journey."

Captain Dana made a grunting sound. "Anybody could guess that, when your own brother is a ship's captain!"

Everyone laughed, but Aunt Harriet insisted it was possible that Maria Castone did possess true extrasensory perception and might be able to help on the mystery of the silver dolphin. "In any case, I suggest you girls call Mr. Howell and tell him what happened."

As soon as they reached home Louise telephoned the trust officer. He was polite, but said firmly, "The reward is going only to a person or persons who find the silver dolphin, and not to someone just giving information that *might* lead to it."

Louise changed the subject. She asked Mr. Howell where Mr. Platt's sister lived and was told that Judy Platt rented an apartment with two other girls in the nearby town of Montville.

"Judy attends Webster College, but she is home on vacation."

"I'd like to meet her," said Louise. "Is that all right with you?"

Mr. Howell said he thought it would be a good idea. "I know you girls will like one another."

Louise obtained the address and directly after lunch she and Jean borrowed their uncle's car and drove to Montville.

Judy Platt proved to be a delightful red-haired girl. She was tall, had small delicate features, and large brown eyes. Even in repose her expression wore a hint of a smile.

"I'm so thrilled to know you're working on this case for Mr. Howell," Judy said, after Louise and Jean had explained the reason for their call. "To tell the truth, I could use some extra money from the sale of the silver dolphin. I'm at college on a scholarship, but I have to do various extra jobs, like baby-sitting, to help out with my expenses."

After Louise and Jean had explained that they were orphans and lived with an aunt and uncle and attended Starhurst School, Judy said, "We have a lot in common. I, too, am an orphan. But unfortunately I don't happen to have a nice aunt and uncle. I have some cousins to whom Oliver left all the available part of his estate. I don't mind, but I do wish I could find out what my brother meant about the silver dolphin."

"You have no idea at all?" Louise asked.

"Not one," Judy answered. "The whole thing is a complete enigma to me. Oliver was twenty years older than I. He always treated me more as if he were my father, but I saw very little of him. He was away most of the time and I didn't even hear from him. Nobody seemed to know where he went or how he got there or back!"

"That is strange," said Jean, feeling sorry for Judy. She perceived that the girl was putting on a brave front. "Well, Louise and I are going to try hard to find your silver dolphin for you."

Judy gave a little giggle. "Maybe you'll find out it's two dolphins," she said. "My brother once said to me in an offhand way he was going to leave me *two* things that were very valuable."

"*Two* things!" Louise exclaimed. "Well, that certainly does complicate matters."

"But only the silver dolphin was mentioned in his will," Jean remarked.

"That's right," said Judy.

She asked the sisters if they themselves had any ideas or had picked up any clues.

Louise smiled. "I don't know whether to call this a clue," she replied, "but do you know a woman in Oak Falls named Maria Castone?"

"I never heard of her," Judy answered. "Who is she?"

Louise explained, then Jean put another question to Judy. "Have you any idea what the stars around your brother's signature mean?"

The girl shook her head.

"We understand your brother inherited some money and gave up his position," Louise went on.

"Yes," said Judy. "He inherited money from Grandfather. Poor me! I was born after Grandfather had died! And my own parents passed away without leaving very much. They had put all their money into some stock which proved to have little value. I've kept the certificates, hoping that someday *maybe* they'll have some value."

Judy's expression had become very sober for a few moments, but her good nature returned and she giggled again. "The certificates are here in my desk. Do you girls want to see what phony securities look like?"

The Danas laughed and said Yes. Judy walked over to a desk, turned the key in the top drawer, and pulled it out. She rummaged inside. Then a strange look came over her face.

The next moment Judy cried out, "They're gone! Somebody has stolen my securities!"

CHAPTER III

A Strange Voice

As Judy stood in dismay before her desk, the Dana girls rushed to her side. They were stunned at her announcement that the stock certificates had been stolen.

"You're sure?" Jean asked Judy.

Judy declared that the securities had been in an envelope at the back of the drawer. "I can't understand why anybody would want to steal them when they're practically worthless."

"Perhaps," said Louise, "they *aren't* worthless. Somebody knew this and took them."

It occurred to Jean that possibly Judy's roommates might know something about the missing stock certificates. She wanted to approach the subject diplomatically and said:

"Who else has access to your desk?"

Judy turned and faced Jean. "My roommates, of course, but they'd never touch a thing!"

"Could they have removed the securities for some reason?" Jean went on.

"I can't see why," Judy replied. She cocked her head as if listening for some special sound. Then she said, "The girls are coming. I know their footsteps."

She went to the door and flung it open. Two attractive girls stood there. "Hi, Judy!" they greeted her, and the shorter of the two asked, "How did everything go today?"

At that moment she and her companion noticed the Danas. The four girls smiled at one another and Judy introduced her apartment mates as Karen Farley and Ruth Nash. The Danas liked them at once. Both were dark-haired, had beautiful complexions, and kind eyes with a straightforward expression in them. Karen was the shorter girl.

Judy told them, "Louise and Jean are amateur detectives. They are going to try and find the silver dolphin for me."

"How exciting!" Ruth exclaimed. "Have you any idea what or where it is?"

"Not yet," Jean replied ruefully.

Suddenly Karen noticed the open desk. "Did you find a clue in there?"

"No," said Judy. "Only hard luck. My envelope with the Master Mining Company stock in it has been stolen!"

Ruth's and Karen's eyes opened wide in astonishment. "Goodness!" Ruth cried out. "When did it happen?"

"It must have been this morning when we were all out," Judy answered, "because I saw the securities in the drawer last night." Then she added, "I was just telling Louise and Jean that the stock was supposed to be practically worthless, but evidently somebody else has other ideas."

"How did the thief get in?" Ruth asked worriedly.

Jean was already examining the front door of the apartment. "The lock has been picked," she said. "There are fresh scratches around the keyhole. We'd better notify the police."

Judy hurried to telephone headquarters. The sergeant on duty assured her he would send two detectives up at once with a fingerprinting kit.

While waiting for the detectives, Judy and her apartment mates thoroughly examined their rooms. They reported that nothing else had been taken or even disturbed.

Judy shrugged and smiled. "I guess the thief figured we girls didn't have anything worth stealing from our costume jewelry boxes!"

In a short time the detectives arrived, took fingerprints of the five girls, then those they found on the desk. After a while, one officer said, "Here are some good prints. From the size it's probably a man's hand. Has any man had access to this desk?"

"No," Judy replied. "At least not since I had it refinished and brought here."

The detective said he had found the prints on the knobs, drawer itself, and places inside. Anyone moving the desk into the room probably wouldn't have touched the inside. "So these prints probably belong to the thief."

The men packed up their kit and told Judy they would give her a report as soon as they learned anything more.

The five girls had an afternoon snack and discussed the mystery of the silver dolphin, then Louise and Jean left.

When the girls reached home they called Mr. Howell and reported what had happened at Judy's apartment. The trust officer was amazed. He thanked them for the information, then added, "There's a lot of that stock in the estate, but it's hardly worth a penny. It's certainly a mystery why anyone would steal the certificates."

Soon dinner was ready. "Smells wonderful!" said Jean. "I'm famished!" She and Louise each had second helpings of delicious roast beef and apple pie.

The mystery of the silver dolphin was discussed at length. Uncle Ned remarked, "I can't figure out what two things could possibly make a silver dolphin."

"And both of them valuable," Jean added. She giggled. "Maybe it's a solid silver dolphin in a solid gold tank!"

Louise grinned. "For myself, I'd rather have a real live dolphin. They're such fun to watch."

"Aye, and that they are," Captain Dana agreed. "They often swim along beside a ship for miles. They can travel at incredible speed. I believe it's as high as sixty miles an hour."

"Whew!" exclaimed Jean. "I certainly wouldn't try to outrace one."

As the meal ended, the telephone rang. Jean answered. The caller was Judy, who cried out excitedly, "The police found out who the thief is! His name is Sensky. The sergeant says he's a town hood, about thirty, medium height, dark-haired. His nickname is Throaty."

"Throaty?" repeated Jean. "How did he get that name?"

Judy explained that the man had a very husky, hoarse voice. "Just as if he had a sore throat or laryngitis."

"Then he should be easy to identify," said Jean. "That's a good clue, Judy. I hope the police catch him soon."

"I doubt they will," Judy told her mournfully. "Nobody seems to know where Throaty is right now."

Jean talked a little more with Judy, urging her not to be discouraged. Then Jean hung up and went to the kitchen, where Aunt Harriet and Louise were already tidying up. Uncle Ned was regluing a chair rung which had fallen off.

The three listened intently as Jean reported Judy's news. "I sure wish I could help you girls on this mystery," Captain Dana said. "Have you any suggestions how I might?"

The sisters thought for a few moments, then Louise answered. "Uncle Ned, could you check with all the shipping lines to learn if Mr. Platt went places by boat and where?"

"That shouldn't be hard," he replied. "I'll get at it first thing in the morning."

"Louise," said Jean, "suppose you and I try checking all the airlines?"

Aunt Harriet looked at her niece in amazement. "You'll have a big job on your hands," she remarked.

"I suppose it is," Louise answered, "but I'm willing to try."

Aunt Harriet said, "You know the old saying, 'All work and no play makes Jack a dull boy.' I suggest that for the next couple of hours we forget all about the mystery and go to the movies. There's an excellent picture I'd like very much to see."

"Then we'll go," said Captain Dana.

The family put on coats and hats and were just ready to leave when the telephone rang. Jean picked up the receiver. "Hello!" she said.

"Is this the Dana house?" a man's hoarse voice inquired.

Jean signaled wildly to Louise as she answered, "Yes, it is." Quickly Jean whispered to her sister,

"Run next door and try to trace this call. I think the person is Throaty Sensky."

Louise was out the door like a shot. The voice at the other end of the wire rasped, "I warn you girls to mind your own business. You understand?"

Jean, stalling for time, countered, "Well, who is this? If I'm to make any such promise, at least I should know who wants it."

She figured that by this time Louise had reached the neighbor's house and had asked the police to trace the call.

"Never mind who this is," the caller retorted.

"But at least tell me how I haven't been minding my own business," Jean went on, determined to keep the suspect on the wire.

She frowned, listening carefully to the answer. "I ain't got any more to say," the hoarse voice replied. "But don't forget what I said. You and your sister had better mind your own business or you'll be sorry!" With that, the caller hung up.

In a couple of minutes Louise returned to the house. She reported having contacted headquarters just too late to find out where the caller was. "I'm sorry." She sighed. "Tell me what Throaty said."

Jean repeated the man's words. Her sister, as well as Aunt Harriet and Uncle Ned, looked worried. Miss Dana at once declared, "I don't like this at all!"

Before she could voice any objection to her

nieces' continuing their detective work, Jean said, "I may have a clue for the police. I'll call them right now." She dialed the number and told the sergeant that while Throaty had been talking to her, she had detected a continuous creaking sound in the background. The officer thanked her and said it might prove to be a helpful clue.

The Dana family left the house and went downtown. The movie proved to be an excellent one, and for the time being, completely dispelled the mystery from their minds.

It was late by the time the four arrived home. As Uncle Ned, who was driving, turned into the driveway, a large object was hurled at him through his half-open window. It hit him on the side of his face, causing him to lose control of the car, which whammed into a tree!

CHAPTER IV

Telltale News Item

THE jolt which the Danas received when their car hit the tree shook them up badly. Louise, in the rear seat with Aunt Harriet, had the presence of mind to look out her window to see who had thrown the object into the car. She saw a man running down the street.

"Who can he be?" she wondered.

Louise knew it would be impossible to overtake the man if she should try chasing him. And unfortunately she had had only a fleeting glimpse of him—hardly enough to give a description to the police.

"Uncle Ned, are you all right?" Jean had cried out quickly.

"Y-yes," he answered. "But the car!"

He opened the door and got out. The girls alighted and came to look at the damaged front end.

"Doesn't seem too serious," Captain Dana said, "but we shouldn't drive the car without having it fixed."

"What was the object that hit you, Uncle Ned?" Louise asked.

"I don't know."

Jean hurried to look at the front seat and brought out a cord-tied roll of newspapers. She put it under her arm to carry into the house.

Louise offered to put the car away and lock the garage. Aunt Harriet advised her brother to get right to bed.

"That was more of a shock to you than you realize," she said. "Oh, yes, I know, you're hale and hearty and used to bumps, but you're only human after all."

The sea captain patted his sister affectionately. "Okay," he said. "First, though, let me call the police and report that man."

By the time Louise had started back to the house, two officers had arrived in a police car and parked in the driveway. They introduced themselves to her as Zotto and Fenwick. Louise led them into the house.

The group sat down in the living room and the Danas told what little they knew about the strange attack. Officer Zotto asked if the family had any idea what the motive of the package thrower might have been.

"I'm afraid not," Aunt Harriet replied. "My

nieces are trying to find the silver dolphin mentioned in Oliver Platt's will. They were present this afternoon when his sister, who lives in Montville, discovered that some securities of hers had been stolen. There may be a connection."

Officer Fenwick nodded. "I also understand from your uncle that Maria Castone has threatened you," he said to Louise and Jean. "All these things may tie in with tonight's incident. Well, we'll work on it and see what we can come up with."

Before leaving, the officers made sure that nothing dangerous was secreted inside the newspapers. Then they said good night. The Danas turned off the lights and went upstairs.

Louise and Jean undressed at once, but Jean, instead of getting into bed, began looking through the newspapers. "There may be a clue in here to that man's identity."

"I'll help," Louise insisted, and took half of the papers. They included recent editions from Oak Falls, Montville, and New York City.

"Of course," Jean admitted, "these papers might not have belonged to the person who threw them."

"Still, it's worth a chance," said Louise.

The young sleuths carefully went over each page to see if there might be any clue—a marked advertisement or news item. Louise discovered nothing and sleepily climbed into bed.

Jean continued her work. She was now perusing

a New York paper and presently came to the financial pages. She was about to skip over them, thinking there could not possibly be a clue in this section, when suddenly her eyes lighted on a news article that startled her. One sentence stood out boldly:

"*It is rumored that there may be activity in the sleeper Master Mining.*"

Jean leaped up and shook Louise who was half asleep. "Listen to this!"

She read the item aloud and then said, "Do you suppose Throaty Sensky saw this? Then, somehow, he found out about Judy's stock. He broke into her apartment and took the securities from the desk. If their value does increase, he'll forge her name and sell them!"

By this time Louise was wide awake again. Jean's theory intrigued her. "You've probably hit on the truth. First thing in the morning we'll do some investigating. But right now, good night. I'm completely exhausted."

Jean laid the papers on the bureau. She turned out the light, raised the shade, and opened a window. Then she jumped into bed and in a short time both girls were sound asleep.

The next morning, as soon as the girls sat down at the breakfast table, they showed the startling newspaper item to Aunt Harriet and Uncle Ned. The captain whistled. "This is quite a find, my hearties," he said. "How do my young detectives expect to use it?"

Louise said first she would like to talk to Mr. Howell. "I'll ask him if he knows about this 'rumor' on the Master Mining stock."

Louise told him the entire story on the phone. The man was amazed.

"I hadn't read about it," he admitted. "You girls are real sleuths all right. I'll look into this matter at once and call you right back."

When he did return Louise's call, Mr. Howell said he had some surprising news for her. "Directly after I talked with you, a New York broker got in touch with me. He wanted to buy the Master Mining stock in the Platt estate. He quoted a good price for it. I told him I would think it over and let him know."

On a hunch, Louise asked Mr. Howell if he would mind finding out from the broker if anyone had offered to sell him Judy Platt's stock. "Jean and I suspect the man who stole her securities may forge her signature."

"You're probably right," he replied. "Here's what I'm going to do. First, call the broker to say Mr. Platt's stock is not for sale. Next, I'll alert the Master Mining Company so they can try to trace anyone attempting to send through a transfer of ownership on Judy's certificates."

Mr. Howell changed the subject and asked Louise how the girls' work was coming along. "Are you any closer to winning the reward for locating the silver dolphin mentioned in the will?"

Louise laughed. "At this point we're pretty baffled," she answered. "We've only been on the case one day and we've already made two enemies —the fortune-teller Maria Castone and Throaty Sensky, a town hood!"

The trust officer chuckled. "That's not bad for a starter," he teased. "Well, I wish you lots of luck."

A little later he telephoned once more, to report that the New York broker had not yet been offered any of Judy's stock. "If the thief is clever, he'll try selling those certificates privately to unsuspecting people. We may never be able to track them down. Sorry to be so discouraging, but that's our opinion."

"Don't all stocks have to be registered?" Louise asked.

"Legally, yes," Mr. Howell agreed, "but people, who don't understand anything about stocks and bonds, might think that all they had to do was take the stock as long as it had been endorsed in the same manner they might endorse a check. They'd pay for it innocently."

"I see," said Louise. "An innocent person could be cheated two ways—he would be buying stolen property, and he wouldn't be able to do anything with it himself because it had not been properly registered."

"That's right," Mr. Howell said.

As soon as the house had been tidied, Uncle

Ned and his nieces took turns on the telephone contacting steamship companies and airlines. They worked for a couple of hours. Not one of the companies who were able to check their records immediately had Oliver Platt listed as having been a passenger during the past year. The larger companies promised to telephone or telegraph collect after checking their passenger lists.

It occurred to Jean and Louise that when Mr. Platt had traveled outside of the United States he might possibly have gone by chartered plane.

"But *where* did he go?" Jean said with a sigh.

"I have a suggestion," Louise spoke up. "Why don't we invite Judy here to lunch, and we can ask her loads of questions about her brother. Maybe from her answers we can get a good clue on where the silver dolphin is."

"That's a grand idea," Jean said. "Will you call her or shall I?"

"You do it."

Judy was delighted to accept the invitation and said she would come by bus to Oak Falls for one-o'clock luncheon.

"Prepare for someone with a big appetite!" she teased.

Uncle Ned had already taken the car to a repair shop which promised to have most of the damage taken care of by lunchtime. Whatever repainting was necessary could be done later. Captain Dana arrived home about twelve-thirty.

"Your skipper's as hungry as a bear," he announced as he walked through the kitchen.

Louise and Jean had been busy setting the table in the dining room and helping Aunt Harriet prepare lunch. They assured their uncle that baked chicken ought to please him.

"And lemon meringue pie," Louise added.

Just before one o'clock the doorbell rang.

"That must be Judy!" said Jean. "I'll get it!"

Both sisters started for the front hall, but before they had gone five steps, a scream of terror came from just outside the door.

"What happened?" Louise cried out.

CHAPTER V

The Dangerous Box

THE screaming continued as the whole Dana family rushed to the front door. Jean yanked it open. Judy Platt, who had been sagging against the door, nearly fell into her arms.

"Judy! What's wrong?" Jean asked quickly.

"Look! Ugh!" Judy pointed to the floor of the porch.

Crawling across the boards was a huge black scorpion!

Louise did not wait to hear more. She dashed into the living room, grabbed up a potted plant, and ran outside. In a moment she had crushed the deadly insect.

"Brave girl!" Uncle Ned boomed out.

Louise took a deep breath. "Where on earth did that repulsive thing come from?"

All eyes turned on Judy and for the first time

they noticed that she held a covered box under one arm.

"I—I was bringing this to you," the girl said shakily, "but I dropped it just as I rang the bell. The lid came off and that—that horrible creature got out."

Louise, Jean and their aunt and uncle exchanged baffled glances.

"Oh, I didn't know what was inside the box!" Judy cried out.

Jean helped the confused, frightened girl into the living room and sat her down in a comfortable upholstered chair. She was completely unnerved and tears glistened in her eyes.

"I'll explain," Judy said in a weak voice. "But first let me put this box down."

"I'll do it," said Jean. She took the box, walked to a picture window, and set it on the sill. Then she seated herself next to Louise near the piano. Aunt Harriet took her usual place by the big window, and Uncle Ned sat in his favorite lounging chair alongside the fireplace.

To ease the tension, Aunt Harriet smiled at the visitor and said, "We haven't had a chance for formal introductions, but I'm sure you're Judy Platt."

"Yes, I am," the girl said. She managed a faint smile. "I'm sorry my first visit here was so scary."

Uncle Ned chuckled. "We're used to the unexpected."

Aunt Harriet went on, "I think a cup of strong tea might be good for Judy. Louise, suppose you run out to the kitchen and make some."

"Thank you," said Judy. "Tea would taste good. First, though, I want to tell you how I happened to bring the box with that awful creature in it.

"While I was dressing to come over here, my buzzer from the lobby sounded. When I answered, a boy's voice said he had a package for me to deliver to the Dana girls. I let him come upstairs and he handed it to me, then went right off. I was afraid I'd be late, so I didn't even bother to put the box in a bag."

As Judy paused, Jean remarked with a grin, "It's a good thing the lid didn't come off in the bus, or you might have had a panic on your hands!"

Again Judy gave a faint smile. "Yes, I guess I was lucky. And lucky too that the lid fell off outdoors, or the scorpion might have bitten whichever of you girls opened the box, and poisoned you!" she said with a shudder.

For some time Uncle Ned had remained silent, his brow furrowed. Finally he said, "What a dastardly thing for anyone to do! Didn't the boy say where the package had come from?"

"Oh, yes, he did," Judy replied. "He said my two apartment mates had sent it."

"Karen and Ruth?" Jean exclaimed.

"Yes. But they'd never play such a hideous trick."

"Of course not," said Louise. "They're wonderful girls." She excused herself to make the tea.

Judy continued to discuss the mystery and gradually seemed to be getting hold of herself. "Somehow I'm sure I'm involved in this horrible episode," she said. "But *how* puzzles me. Have you Danas any idea?"

Jean spoke up. "I wonder if Maria Castone could have done it."

Aunt Harriet asked, "What makes you suspect her?"

Jean admitted that maybe her idea was wrong, but she always connected scorpions with warm places and especially Spanish-speaking countries. "Perhaps Maria had faraway friends or relatives send the scorpions to her. It would not surprise me if she kept a few to frighten people."

"How awful!" Judy exclaimed.

Captain Dana commented, "If you are right, Jean, then she must have a spy who found out Judy was coming here."

By this time Louise had brewed the tea and was on her way back to the living room. As she walked in, her eyes suddenly grew large in terror.

"Aunt Harriet, jump up!" she gasped.

Without hesitation Miss Dana obeyed, and everyone looked to see the reason for Louise's warning.

A scorpion was crawling over the back of the chair which Aunt Harriet had just vacated!

Judy screamed and leaped away from her own chair. Uncle Ned, meanwhile, had grabbed up a fireplace tool and soon ended the scorpion's life. He shoveled up its remains and took them outdoors.

Jean had yanked Aunt Harriet's chair from the window, thinking there might be more scorpions in the box. Then she discovered that the box had fallen off the window sill, probably because the creature's movements had unbalanced it, and the lid had opened.

A piece of paper padding indicated that the second scorpion had been underneath it, and so had not escaped before. Jean pointed out that there were no other deadly insects around.

Uncle Ned looked relieved and said, "We can all sit down now and stop worrying."

"I'm worried just the same," Aunt Harriet told him. "When I think of what might have happened to Louise and Jean, it makes me shiver."

Jean heaved a sigh. "At least the person who donated these poisonous creatures wasn't stingy— one bug for Louise and one for me!"

Louise, realizing that her sister was trying to calm everyone's nerves by her facetious remark, added, "And now we have none!"

She handed a cup of steaming, fragrant tea to Judy, then went to examine the box and the paper. There was no clue of any kind on the box itself about the sender. It was white and plain and a couple of tiny holes had been punched in one side,

"Aunt Harriet, jump up!" Louise gasped

apparently to give air to the scorpions. Louise now picked up the layer of paper, which she looked at carefully and then turned over.

"Oh, my goodness!" she exclaimed.

"What is it?" the others chorused.

Louise held up the paper for everyone to see. On it four stars had been drawn in ink exactly the way they had appeared around Oliver Platt's signature!

The discovery had a violent effect on Judy. She began to cry hysterically. "My brother's special insignia!" she sobbed. "Oh, how could he be mixed up in this?"

Louise and Jean went to her side and patted the girl affectionately on her shoulders.

"There must be some explanation. If your brother did make these stars," Louise said kindly, "someone else got hold of the paper."

"Oh, I don't know what to think!" Judy answered woefully.

Aunt Harriet urged the distraught girl to drink her tea. She began to sip it. The Danas remained silent to give her time to compose herself.

All were very puzzled. One thing was certain. The paper was a sinister warning to the Dana girls that they were facing danger in trying to solve the Platt mystery.

Wisely, the whole family decided that for Judy's sake they should change the subject. They winked at one another as a signal.

Captain Dana started the conversation by asking Judy what courses she was taking at college. Instantly she became interested in giving him full details. Judy also talked about a summer camp where she had worked.

"If you'll excuse me," said Aunt Harriet presently, "I'll put lunch on the table."

All through the meal Judy talked animatedly with her new friends on various topics. She laughed a good bit and proved to be a very humorous and interesting conversationalist.

Near the end of the meal, it occurred to Louise and Jean that the reason they had invited Judy to their home was to question her about her brother and possibly get a clue from which to proceed on the mystery. At the moment the reward for finding the silver dolphin seemed a long way off! Besides, reward or not, they were eager to help Judy locate her inheritance.

It was Judy herself who surprisingly brought up the subject. "I've been thinking how I could help solve the dolphin mystery," she said. "Something occurred to me about my brother that may be a real clue!"

CHAPTER VI

Blizzard Bound

EVERYONE listened intently as Judy began her story.

"From the time I was a little girl, I remember that my brother was positively nuts on the subject of stars. He had all kinds of books on astronomy and telescopes and even took up the subject of astrology."

Captain Dana smiled. "Then I can see how he adopted the habit of putting stars around his signature."

Suddenly Louise had an idea. She excused herself from the table and went to the living room for a volume of the encyclopedia. In a few minutes she returned.

"My hunch has paid off!" she said excitedly. "Listen to this!"

Louise read a few sentences which stated there

was a constellation named Delphinus. "That's Latin for dolphin!" she said, looking up. "And there's more to it. The constellation is sometimes pictured as containing four stars—three in a semicircle and another one below the third star."

Captain Dana chuckled. "Good for you, Louise! I've known about the Delphinus constellation for years, but it would take somebody like you with a detective's mind to put two and two together."

"It's a marvelous discovery," said Judy. "But how does it help me find my silver dolphin?" She giggled. "It wouldn't do me much good if it's up in the sky!"

No one could even make a guess in answer to her question. Their elation of a few moments before turned to a feeling of being completely stymied. Apparently there was a correlation between the constellation and Oliver Platt's strange signature and bequest to Judy.

Finally Louise said, "Maybe we'll get a clue in the section on dolphins."

She quickly found the right place. The others listened intently as Louise read the article. It told how people in ancient times used the dolphin in their art. Greeks and Romans particularly showed great affection for this sea mammal. It was gentle, playful, and highly intelligent.

Louise went on reading. " 'The dolphin is often found on antique coins, mural paintings, furniture and utensils and ornaments, and for decorations in architecture. During ancient times, and even today, the dolphin enjoys a kind of respect that protects it from persecution.' "

When she finished reading, Louise said, "I love the part that told of there being many cases on record where the dolphin has proved to be a life-saver and rescued drowning people. I suppose they clung to one of the fins and were pulled to shore."

Aunt Harriet remarked, "That legend about the first white man visiting South America and arriving on the back of a sea beast is very interesting. I suppose he may have been a shipwrecked sailor riding on top of a dolphin."

Everyone was intrigued by the fact that it had now been determined through experiments that the dolphin makes sixty different sounds, giving it a rather extensive vocabulary for a creature of the sea.

"And I think it's fascinating," said Judy, "that the dolphin's built-in sonar is not only extremely useful to him, but also of great value to scientists who are studying just how sonar works."

Judy went on to say that she remembered vividly when as a child she had taken one of her brother's books and had crayoned all the pictures in it of dolphins. "Boy, did he scold me!"

Everyone laughed and then became serious as Judy went on, "Maybe Oliver left me a live silver-colored dolphin. If he did, I suppose it would be pretty valuable."

"I'm sure it would be," said Captain Dana.

The red-haired girl remarked that she could not get out of her mind, however, what her brother had told her—that he was leaving her *two* valuable things.

"But in his will he didn't say silver dolphins, so it couldn't possibly be two of them. What in the world could the other thing be?"

"If we could answer that," Jean said with a chuckle, "we'd have this mystery solved. But I do have a suggestion."

"What is it?" Judy asked eagerly.

"Suppose your brother had found a live silver dolphin," Jean answered. "Where would he have kept it?" When Judy did not reply, Jean said, "Why, in an oceanarium, of course."

"You're right!" Judy agreed. "But where is that oceanarium? My brother traveled a lot, so it could be most anywhere in the world!"

Jean admitted that the riddle would not be easy to figure out, but she added, "Why don't we get in touch with as many oceanariums as possible and ask if any of them are boarding a silver dolphin?"

Louise had noted that there was a list of United States oceanariums in her uncle's Marine Encyclopedia. "We can send them telegrams and ask that the answers be sent collect."

"A splendid idea," Uncle Ned remarked.

A message was composed and sent off to the list of names in the encyclopedia.

"How soon do you think we'll get replies?" Judy asked.

"That's a good question," Jean answered. "But we'll let you know the minute we hear anything."

A short time later Judy said she must leave for home. As she was putting on her coat, Aunt Harriet remarked, "It started to snow an hour or so ago. Louise and Jean, you'd better drive Judy to the bus."

At once Louise said, "We'll drive her all the way home. Then we'll have more time to discuss the mystery with Judy." She smiled. "Every time Judy talks about her brother, I learn something more. She's full of clues!"

The others laughed.

"Very well. Go ahead, but be careful on the slippery streets," Aunt Harriet warned.

The girls found that the snow was coming down hard and fast. By the time they reached Montville, there were three inches on the ground and the storm seemed to be getting worse.

As Judy alighted from the car, she said, "I'd invite you girls in for a bite, but I'm afraid your aunt and uncle will be worried if you don't get home as soon as possible."

"You're right," said Jean. " 'Bye now. We'll be talking to you soon."

"Good luck!" Judy called as Louise drove off.

By this time the late-afternoon sky had darkened,

and the storm was now a raging blizzard. The wind
blew so hard that Louise had difficulty bucking it.
At times the car shivered and would have been
blown to the opposite lane if Louise had not held a
firm grip on the wheel.

The windshield wiper was zipping back and
forth furiously, but despite this, it was difficult to
see very far ahead. Louise had turned on the head-
lights and the car was moving along the highway
at a slow pace.

"This is awful!" Jean said presently. "Oh—look
out!"

A reckless driver, with no lights on, had whizzed
toward them and swerved barely in time to keep
from hitting the Dana car.

"Wow! I hope we don't meet any more crazy
drivers like that one!" Jean exclaimed.

Louise did not reply. Her mind was completely
on the road and her driving.

In a short time they came to a long stretch of
open country. Here the wind had piled the snow
into small drifts and Louise found it necessary to
skirt several of them to keep the car from becoming
stuck in one.

Jean remarked, "Funny, we haven't seen a car
coming from the opposite direction in a long
time."

She did not say it aloud, but Jean wondered if
perhaps there were some blockade or accident
ahead.

A short time later a strange look came over Louise's face. Her sister noticed it and said, "What's the matter?"

"The car is acting strangely," Louise answered. "It's slowing down, and no matter how much gas I give it, the engine won't make any speed."

Jean looked quickly at the fuel gauge on the dashboard. "We have plenty of gas. Something else is the matter."

Within less than a minute the engine died. Louise tried over and over again to start it, but her endeavors were futile.

"I guess we'll have to go for help," she said, opening the car door.

Jean got out of the other side and the sisters started trudging up the road. The wind cut their faces and the snow almost blinded them.

"It's going to be a long walk!" Jean remarked. "There isn't a house on this road for at least another mile."

Louise nodded. She had turned so her back was against the wind, but a sudden terrific gust knocked her over. Jean helped her stand up and the two struggled on. Seconds later another blast of the gale, together with slippery footing, sent both girls headlong.

"It's no use!" said Louise, getting up. "We'll have to return to the car."

"There won't be any heat. We can't just sit there in the cold," Jean remarked.

"Anything would be better than bucking this storm," said Louise, turning back.

Jean followed, torn between a desire to get to a warm place and the realization that Louise was right. After a great deal of difficulty, the girls reached the car. They got in and sat down. By this time the automobile was blanketed with snow and they could not even see outside.

"Louise," said Jean, "we're really in a mess! Do you realize we may be snowed under?"

CHAPTER VII

Shower of Doughnuts

DESPERATE, Louise tried starting the motor of the car once more. No response.

"I wonder what's the matter with it," she said, disgusted.

"It could be one of any number of things," Jean remarked. "But one thing I do know—the heating system should be on a battery so it could be turned off and on even if the motor is dead. Then we wouldn't have to sit here and freeze."

"I wish I could see out," Louise complained. "Let's brush the snow off the windows."

The girls scooped up snow brushes from the floor of the rear seat and stepped outside. It did not take long to remove the snow, but five minutes later the windows were covered again.

"It's no use," Jean said disconsolately. She began stamping her feet and swinging her arms to get warm.

The sisters fell into dejected silence, but presently Louise tried the horn to attract attention.

"Maybe it will summon help," she said hopefully.

Louise pressed the horn continuously for half a minute, then waited. She kept up this routine, but not a person or car appeared.

"I guess nobody is coming out in this storm," Jean said finally.

"At any rate," Louise observed, "the sound of the horn is practically muffled with this terrible wind blowing."

Half an hour had gone by when the girls became aware of the dim glow of lights through the snowy rear window. Louise blew the horn furiously. There was a friendly response from a vehicle behind them.

"Saved!" exclaimed Jean.

She opened her door and stepped into the snow, which was now a foot deep. Louise climbed out the other side.

The sisters could see a large truck with a snowplow in front. It pulled up close to them and the driver leaned out.

"You in trouble?" he called.

"We sure are," Jean replied. "Our car won't start. The engine has failed."

The driver of the snow truck was a large, ruddy-faced, good-natured man. "That's tough luck," he said. "I'll see if I can help you out. Where do you come from?"

"Oak Falls."

The man whistled. "You're several miles from home. Well, let's try an experiment. I'll shovel the snow away from around your car, then I'll start pushing you. After you get rolling, maybe the engine will catch."

"Thanks a million," said Louise.

The girls climbed back into their car and waited while the driver "shoveled them out." Then they helped him clean off the hood, windshield, and the other windows. "Now we're ready," the man said, and attached a wheelless tire to the front of the truck, so that it was at the same height as the Danas' bumper, and he drove up close to the car. Soon the girls felt an impact.

Louise steered as their rescuer pushed and pushed. Each time the car gathered a little momentum Louise would put it into gear to see if the engine would catch. This procedure went on for nearly a mile with no results.

The sisters were about to abandon all hope of driving the car home, when suddenly there was a sound from the motor, the car gave a jerk, and the next moment the engine was running smoothly.

"Hurray!" Jean shouted.

Louise did not dare stop, even to thank the man with the snowplow. But presently he began to toot his horn. She slowed down until he came abreast of her.

"I'll go ahead of you and cut a path," he shouted. "You may come to a big drift you can't get through."

He closed the window through which he had been talking and pulled ahead. Louise followed close on the rear of the big truck. She found the going much easier over the newly plowed road.

Their benefactor went all the way to the outskirts of Oak Falls. Here, he stopped and Louise pulled past him. Jean lowered the window on her side and shouted the girls' appreciation.

"Safe home!" he called out, a big grin on his face.

The streets of Oak Falls had been plowed, and the girls experienced little trouble reaching the Dana home. Even their own driveway had been shoveled, evidently by Uncle Ned, using the family's small snow blower. But it was still storming and the girls knew the job would have to be done again in the morning.

"I'll bet Uncle Ned did this shoveling just so we could get the car in the garage," said Louise.

He and Aunt Harriet swooped the two girls into their arms, saying how relieved they were to see them home safely.

"We were terribly worried," Miss Dana remarked. "What kept you so long?"

Her nieces quickly explained; then she shooed them off to take hot showers and change into warm clothes. When the girls came downstairs, they caught the aroma of delicious homemade vegetable soup and steaks sizzling on the broiler.

"Judy called," Aunt Harriet said. "She was very worried about your getting home. In fact, she has phoned three times. You ought to call her right away and let her know you arrived safely."

Louise went to the phone and dialed the red-haired girl's number.

"Oh, I'm so relieved to hear from you," Judy said. "The storm got so much worse after you left me. Well, thanks for calling and I'm glad you made it all right. Be seeing you."

As Louise hung up, Aunt Harriet called the family to the table. During the meal Uncle Ned told his nieces that the telephone had been ringing constantly since they had left. "One message and telegram after another. Several steamship and airlines sent wires. They have made a thorough search, but have no record of having had a passenger named Oliver Platt."

"Too bad," Louise remarked.

Then Aunt Harriet spoke up. "One of the phone calls was from Maria Castone," Miss Dana said. "She was very sweet and ingratiating. I can't see why you girls feel that she may be a dangerous person. After all, we can't prove she sent the scorpions. I think she's just temperamental."

Uncle Ned gave a snort. "Temperamental, eh? I'd say that anybody who threatens my nieces and puts an unlucky sign on them *is* a dangerous person!"

Aunt Harriet shrugged. "Well, anyhow, she wanted Louise or Jean to get in touch with her—said she had something very important to tell them."

Captain Dana chuckled. "She just said that to keep their curiosity aroused. I'd like to bet she's going to cause you girls more trouble. I wouldn't pay any attention to her."

Louise and Jean laughed, and Jean said, "Uncle Ned, you're an old dear and you certainly size people up well. But do you really think we should ignore Maria Castone?" Jean winked at him. "You know, she *is* a fortune-teller!"

"Oh, well, go ahead," her uncle conceded.

Jean dashed to the telephone and dialed Maria. At first the woman acted disgruntled that the girl had not called sooner. Jean explained the reason— the trip to Montville and the storm.

Angrily the fortune-teller said, "You should have nothing more to do with Judy Platt. This blizzard should teach you a lesson. I have warned you that great danger will come to you Dana girls if you do not leave the Platt case alone."

Jean bristled. "I think that's for my sister and me to decide."

"All right," said Maria Castone. "You do as you

like, but never claim that you weren't told the truth by one who knows. And now, I will tell you why I wanted to talk to you."

Becoming very dramatic in tone, Maria went on, "Last night I had a dream. In it I could see Mr. Platt bringing me the silver dolphin."

"Some dream!" Jean giggled.

Maria Castone paid no attention to the remark. "I have analyzed this dream from every angle," she said. "I interpret it to mean that you and your sister will never discover the silver dolphin, so my advice to you is to give up trying!"

"I can't promise that," said Jean. "But thank you anyway for telling me about your dream." She hung up.

When Jean rejoined her family, she cried out, "The nerve of that woman!" Then she told her story.

Uncle Ned laughed. "I said all along she was a fake. I'll bet she concocted that dream—just for the benefit of my nieces."

Aunt Harriet looked solemn. "I'm not so sure that Maria is not psychic," she said. "Don't forget that since she warned you of danger, you two girls have been having more than a bit of bad luck."

"Aye, they have," said Captain Dana. "But not because of what Maria said. And here's my advice to you, my hearties—get to bed early."

The sisters were only too glad to do this. They

were very weary from their long, eventful day. But not too weary to spend a few minutes in speculation. What was Maria Castone's motive? What lay behind her warnings? Was it self-interest, or did she know more than she was telling and was really trying to protect them?

"I can't believe she has any personal interest in our safety," Jean declared.

"And I agree," said Louise. "The interest is all in herself!" Then she added, "I'm afraid the woman is dangerous. We must watch our step."

Both girls were sound asleep the next morning when Louise was aroused by a loud pounding on the front door.

"Who can that be?" she asked herself.

By this time Jean had heard the noise and was wide awake. Puzzled, the sisters put on robes and slippers, then hurried down the stairs. By this time Aunt Harriet had appeared and in a few moments Uncle Ned followed.

Louise flung open the front door. Amid a swirling gust of white flakes, a young woman, disheveled and covered with snow, stumbled inside.

"Applecore!" Louise and Jean cried out.

This was the nickname Jean had given the Danas' maid Cora Appel. The frowzy-looking girl, her purse dangling on one arm and a bulky shopping bag clutched in her other hand, took a few steps forward. Suddenly she slipped, and before anyone could grab her, went tumbling headfirst along the hall.

Cora's purse flew in one direction and the contents of the shopping bag shot out in every direction. A dozen doughnuts showered onto the four Danas!

CHAPTER VIII

An Exciting Telegram

ALTHOUGH Louise and Jean burst into laughter, they nevertheless felt sorry for Cora and hurried to help the girl. Her spill was no surprise to the Danas. Applecore was clumsy, often tripping and bumping into furniture. She always had bruises on some part of her body!

Cora never reacted quickly and this time was no exception. She lay sprawled on the floor and began to sniffle.

Louise and Jean assisted her to a sitting position. "Are you hurt?" they asked.

They received the usual answer, "No." Cora went on in a plaintive tone, "I was bringin' you somethin' nice and now look! The doughnuts are ruined!"

"Maybe not," Louise said kindly. "We'll brush them off thoroughly and resugar them. I'm sure they're delicious, and we'll eat every one down to the last crumb."

Her encouraging words prompted Cora to rise to her feet. Aunt Harriet and Uncle Ned had stood by, looking on sympathetically.

Now Miss Dana spoke up. "Cora, you were brave to come to work today in all this snow."

Suddenly Cora's pride asserted itself. She had often said she loved working for the Danas, and now cried out, as if she had been insulted, "I got to shovel snow, don't I? What am I hired for? Not to stay home!"

Without another word she picked up the doughnuts and various packages which had spilled from the shopping bag and made her way to the kitchen.

Louise and Jean helped her brush off the doughnuts and resugar them. Then Cora resolutely went out the back door and waded through the drifts to the garage for a snow shovel. It was clear now and the sun spread a glow over the still white scene.

"Isn't it beautiful out?" Louise murmured.

Uncle Ned said he would dress and go outside himself to use the snow blower.

"Louise and I will help too," Jean offered. "We'll shovel the walks by hand."

The sisters dressed quickly and joined Cora, who was alternately sweeping and shoveling snow from the front porch. In the meantime, Uncle Ned had the blower roaring along the driveway.

As Louise and Jean worked side by side with Cora, the three discussed the weather.

"The forecast isn't good," Cora remarked. "Says more snow."

Louise nodded and remarked to Jean, "This'll sure slow down our sleuthing."

"What?" exclaimed Cora, almost dropping her shovel. "You girls aren't on another case?"

Louise and Jean laughed. "Yes, we are," Louise said. "And a very interesting and unusual one, too."

Cora gave a shudder. The Danas guessed what was going through her mind. Cora had had several terrifying experiences when the girls had been working on the *Mystery of the Stone Tiger*. After the last such incident, she had vowed never again to become involved in any of their cases.

Cora did not allude to this, but said, "You know what I think? That they shouldn't teach you at that fancy boardin' school you go to how to be detectives!"

The Danas howled with laughter. The thought of their stern headmistress allowing a course in sleuthing was so funny they kept bursting into giggles every few minutes as they shoveled.

"I don't see what's so funny about that," Cora said finally. "Why, if you keep on detectin', one of these days you're goin' to get into real, terrible trouble!"

Jean impishly could not refrain from saying, "I

guess we're already in danger. A fortune-teller has put an unlucky sign on both Louise and me."

"Oh, no!" Cora cried, and this time she dropped the broom she was using. "Well, I'm awful sorry for you. Please, don't do a mite more detectin'. I don't want anything to happen to you. You're—you're too nice!"

Louise patted the worried girl on one shoulder. "Don't worry, Cora," she said, "Jean and I will watch our step."

But Jean's teasing had evidently upset Apple-core. She stood twisting her hands and biting her lips.

"Oh, cheer up," said Louise. "It's not as bad as Jean pictures it. We'll be all right."

In a short time all the snow shoveling had been finished and the four workers trooped into the kitchen. Here a new shock awaited Cora. Aunt Harriet had a steaming hot breakfast ready.

The maid, instead of being pleased, was close to tears. "Miss Dana," she said, "you didn't have to do that. It's my job. Maybe I don't do it as well as you do, but that's what you pay me for."

Once more Cora had to be comforted, but her spirits rose as she consumed orange juice, a bowl of hot cereal, bacon and eggs, and a doughnut.

The family had barely finished eating when a telegram arrived for the girls. Louise opened the message which was a response from an oceanarium in California. It was disappointing. No one there had ever had any dealings with a man named Oliver Platt, nor were they "boarding" a dolphin for him. During the morning other similar wires came.

"Well, I guess that idea won't produce a clue," Jean remarked with a huge sigh.

The next telegram received by the Danas had been sent from Miami and had a different tenor. The message was:

BELIEVE CAN HELP YOU IF YOU COME HERE.

At once Louise and Jean became excited. "We're on the right track!" Jean exclaimed, her eyes sparkling with renewed hopes of finding the silver dolphin.

The girls ran to tell their aunt and uncle. "Listen to this!" Jean said, and repeated the message. "Do you think it would be possible for you to take Louise and me to Miami?"

"Miami?" Uncle Ned blinked. "That's a long way from here." He chuckled. "I know you girls want to win that reward, but I don't believe I can take off that much time."

"And I'm tied up with several projects I've promised to work on for certain charities," said Aunt Harriet. "I'm sorry. Besides, it would be rather expensive for all of us to go."

"Aye, that it would, my hearties," said Uncle Ned, "but I'll see what I can do."

"We understand," said Louise. "As to the reward, I have forgotten about that. My main thought now is to help Judy get her inheritance."

"I'm with you," Jean said earnestly.

"And I'd like to help her," said Uncle Ned, beaming at his nieces.

Louise urged that they notify Judy at once about the message from Miami. When the red-haired girl heard it, she squealed in ecstasy.

"Now we're getting some place!" she exclaimed. "Let's go there!"

When Louise gently hinted at the problem of expense, Judy replied, "My college roommate, Anne Erskine, lives in Miami. I'm sure she'd be thrilled to have all of us stay with her."

Judy giggled. "It wouldn't cost us anything but plane fare!"

"Staying with Anne sounds marvelous!" said Louise. "But are you sure it would be all right?"

Judy's voice came over the wire excitedly. "Anne has been begging me to spend part of the Christmas holidays with her. And guess what? In today's mail came a Christmas check from one of my cousins who is a beneficiary under my brother's will. That would take care of my transportation."

Louise asked Judy to hold on while she spoke to her aunt and uncle. They quickly consented to the plan and Louise went back to the phone jubilant.

"It's okay here!" she said. "You find out from Anne if her parents want us. If they do, let's go as soon as possible. We'll get plane reservations."

Judy soon received an affirmative answer. "My roommate is positively delirious at the idea of our coming to visit and solving a mystery!"

"I hope we can solve it," said Louise. She told Judy about Maria Castone's dream. "We all think that fortune-teller made it up, but Jean and I want to go downtown and talk to her again before we leave."

Uncle Ned attended to the reservations and secured them for a Florida flight the following afternoon. Louise called Judy to tell her this and she in turn said she would get in touch with Anne and tell her. There was now a flurry of excitement as the sisters brought down suitcases from the attic and packed them with clothes appropriate for Miami temperatures.

Later that afternoon the Dana girls hopped a bus downtown. Uncle Ned had taken the car back to the repair garage to have the repainting job done. When the sisters walked into Maria Castone's studio, she greeted them politely, but was very cool.

When they asked the fortune-teller about the dream, she said, "Mr. Platt was a client of mine. He didn't come here very often, since he was out of the country a great deal. But he was an expert on the subject of stars and we loved to talk about them."

Louise asked Maria if she thought there could be any connection between the missing silver dolphin and the constellation Delphinus. The fortune-teller did not answer for a minute.

Finally she said, "I suppose there could be. I will concentrate on the subject."

Jean felt it was useless to pursue the matter, so she asked suddenly, "Maria, since you're so clairvoyant, can you tell my sister and me where a man named Throaty Sensky is?"

The fortune-teller jerked up in her chair to a rigid position. She lowered her eyelids until her eyes were mere slits. "Who wants to know?" she snapped.

Jean became wary. Assuming indifference, she shrugged. "Just curious. I understand he's wanted by the police."

Maria opened her eyes again. Now they were blazing. "Then let the police come and ask me!" she shouted. "I have nothing more to say! Good day!"

She arose and disappeared into a back room.

CHAPTER IX

Treasure Chair

On the way home Louise and Jean discussed Maria Castone's peculiar reaction to Jean's mention of Throaty Sensky.

"She acted almost guilty," Louise commented. "Do you suppose there could be any connection between the two? It seems funny she'd be friends with a thief, unless there's something brewing."

"Search me," Jean replied. "Let's stop at police headquarters and tell them about Maria's remarks. After what she said about the police, they may want to talk to her themselves."

The sisters told their story to the sergeant on duty. After some thought he smiled. "It's my guess that Throaty is a client of Maria Castone and she is trying to protect him.

"Incidentally, the Montville police have not picked up a single clue to Throaty's whereabouts. It would be quite a feather in our cap here in Oak

Falls if we could locate him!" The officer grinned broadly.

The sisters agreed, wishing they themselves could track down the suspect! Later, at home, the girls discussed the elusive Throaty with their aunt and uncle.

"It's a shame," said Uncle Ned, "that the good clue you gave the police about hearing a continuous creaking sound in the background didn't help them any. Suppose I give that clue a try myself and see what I can come up with."

Louise and Jean looked at the captain in amazement. Louise said, "That's great, Uncle Ned. How will you go about it?"

"The best way to find a suspect," Captain Dana replied, "is to learn who his pals are and where they live."

Aunt Harriet asked, "Wouldn't the police know that?"

Her brother admitted that they probably would, and no doubt had already interrogated Throaty's friends. "But a crook's pals rarely reveal anything about him to the police."

"True. What is your plan of attack, Uncle Ned?" Jean asked eagerly.

"To see if I can find out who Throaty's best friend is."

Uncle Ned said that he had a close friend in Montville who was a retired sea captain. "Through people around the docks, a seafaring man can pick up a good bit of information about what's going on in town, including anything of a shady nature."

"That's a wonderful idea!" said Jean. "Uncle Ned, could you start right away?"

Captain Dana grinned. "I knew you'd ask me that. Well, I offered to help, so I might as well get going."

He strode to the telephone and put a call in to his old friend. When he rejoined his family, Uncle Ned was beaming. He said, "Sam was tickled to death to get the assignment. He'll call me back if he learns anything."

An hour later, when the phone rang, Uncle Ned jumped to answer it. As he listened to the caller, a broad smile spread over Captain Dana's face.

Louise and Jean, who were looking on, exchanged glances. The news was good! They listened avidly as their uncle remarked:

"You say his name is Bengler and he lives at 69 Regency Street? . . . Fine. . . . Sam, you haven't changed a bit. Give you a job to do and you go right to it. I always said you were as good a detective as you were a sea captain!" Uncle Ned laughed.

After a little more conversation, he hung up. Louise and Jean rushed to his side and hugged him.

Aunt Harriet, who had been listening in a more

placid frame of mind, smiled and said, "I suppose you'll all be going over to Montville to hunt up this man Bengler."

"We sure will!" said Uncle Ned. "Girls, get your snow gear on and we'll be off. The car's all fixed now."

Aunt Harriet had a suggestion. "Since driving conditions still aren't good, why don't you girls see if Judy can come back here with you and spend the night?"

"That's a great idea," said Jean. "Then we won't have to worry about her being delayed tomorrow. It would be awful to miss our plane to New York."

Louise called Judy, who said she would be ready when the Danas came for her. She was excited about the sleuthing they planned in tracking down Throaty's friend.

"But don't get hurt or captured so we can't go to Florida tomorrow!" she warned before hanging up, and Louise promised.

Captain Dana, in the meantime, had gone upstairs. He now returned to the living room wearing his ship's uniform. His sister and the girls looked at him in surprise.

"I thought maybe if I wore this, nobody would be suspicious of my motives. In street clothes I might be mistaken for a detective or a plain-clothesman!"

The others laughed. When Louise and Jean were

dressed in ski jackets and boots and ready to leave, Aunt Harriet wished the three luck. They went out the door, chatting gaily.

As they rode along, with Uncle Ned at the wheel, the girls speculated on how much they might be able to find out from Bengler.

When they reached Montville, Uncle Ned asked a policeman directions to Regency Street. The Danas quickly found the apartment house at Number 69, parked the car, and rang Bengler's bell.

A buzzer unlocked the front door. The trio walked down the hall and knocked on 14-A. The knock was answered by a small, wiry man with shifty eyes.

"Yes?"

The Danas knew at once he was suspicious of his callers, but Uncle Ned tried to allay this. With a little chuckle he said, "Howdy, Mr. Bengler! Guess you don't know me. But the girls and I were wondering if you could help us. I have something for a friend of yours. May we come in?"

Grudgingly Bengler opened the door wider so that his visitors might enter. He sat down first and the others took chairs.

"Well, talk." Bengler's manner was not friendly.

Captain Dana was not intimidated. "When you travel the seven seas as I do," he said easily, "you pick up a lot of information and people ask you to do a lot of favors. Right now I've been asked by someone to get in touch with Throaty Sensky. I understand you are a friend of his. You're just the person to help me."

Bengler retorted, "If you've got somethin' for him, why don't you leave it with me? I haven't seen him lately, but once or twice a year he stops in here."

The Danas realized that they were not going to get any information from the man. He appeared rather nervous, however, and began to rock back and forth in his chair. It was an old-fashioned rocker, with a cushion tied on over the seat. The chair creaked continuously.

Louise and Jean exchanged quick glances. Each was thinking, could this possibly have been the creaking sound heard by Jean over the telephone when Throaty had called their home and threatened the girls?

As Jean's eyes roamed the room, she saw a telephone on a table. To herself she said, "It's at just about the right distance to pick up the creaking noise. Perhaps Throaty had called from here. While he was talking, Bengler might have been rocking back and forth in his pet chair."

Her gaze wandered over to the man and she studied the chair more closely. The cushion was tied on at each corner of the seat. Suddenly a wild hunch came to her.

"Mr. Bengler," she said, smiling sweetly, "I just adore old-fashioned rockers. Would you mind ter-

"Here are the stolen securities!" Jean cried out

ribly letting me sit in yours for a few moments?"

Bengler seemed startled by the request and acted at first as if he was not going to grant it.

But finally he stood up and said, "All right. Go ahead."

Louise and Uncle Ned wondered what Jean had in mind. They had an intuitive feeling that their part in the act was to keep Bengler's attention away from Jean. At once both of them began to talk about a picture which hung on the opposite wall of the room.

Jean, in the meantime, rocked back and forth as if she were having a wonderful time. Actually she was busily untying the tapes on the two rear corners of the cushion. When she succeeded in loosening them, Jean started to stand up. As if it had happened accidentally, she pulled the cushion up with her. It flopped forward and she stared at the wooden seat.

On it, neatly arranged, lay several certificates of Master Mining stock! Judy Platt's name was inscribed on them!

Jean gasped and cried out, "Here are the stolen securities!" She quickly snatched up one of the papers.

The others had turned quickly at Jean's announcement. Now Uncle Ned made a grab for Bengler. But the man moved too fast for capture. He yanked open the door to his apartment and in a second was running down the hall!

Captain Dana said tersely to his nieces, "Take those certificates to our car. Wait for me there. I'll try to catch Bengler!"

"Let me go with you," Jean begged.

"No. Guarding those papers is more important."

Uncle Ned dashed into the corridor after the fugitive. Louise and Jean, disappointed that they could not join the chase, let him go.

Louise gathered up the securities, and they hurried off to the car. The sisters waited, growing more restless as time went by. After half an hour had elapsed with no sign of Uncle Ned, they were worried.

"I wonder what's happened," said Louise. "It's a pretty long chase!"

"Yes," Jean agreed. "Oh, I hope nothing has happened to Uncle Ned!"

CHAPTER X

Captain Dana's Chase

AFTER another fifteen minutes of anxious waiting, Louise said to Jean, "Maybe Uncle Ned had to chase Bengler some distance from here, and phoned home to leave a message for us saying he's okay."

"That's possible," Jean replied. "Why don't you call up and find out? I'll stand guard here."

Louise hurried off to an outside phone booth. But a few minutes later her hopes faded. Aunt Harriet answered and said she had not heard from her brother.

Now she too was worried and Louise chided herself for alarming her aunt, who said, "Call me up as soon as you hear anything."

"All right. And if I don't have any news about Uncle Ned, I'll call you, anyway."

Louise then returned to Jean. As the girls were discussing what their next move should be, a police squad car with two officers pulled up alongside them and stopped.

An officer poked his head out the window and called, "Are you the Dana girls?"

"Yes, we are," Louise replied.

The sisters' hearts began to pound. Were they about to receive bad news?

"We came to take you to headquarters," the officer said. "Follow us."

"All right," Louise said, "but why are we going?"

"Because Captain Dana and a prisoner are there."

"Oh, thank goodness!" the two girls chorused, and Louise added, "Is our Uncle Ned all right?"

The officer, who said his name was Runcie, smiled. "Fit as a fiddle, and I might say, rather proud to have captured the man who ran away from you people."

"You mean Bengler?" Jean inquired.

Officer Runcie nodded. "Your uncle wouldn't give up the chase. He went zigzagging through town after Bengler like a hound dog. He finally trailed him to a drugstore where Bengler had gone to phone. Then Captain Dana rushed out to tell a patrolman on duty at an intersection. He came back and arrested Bengler."

The Dana girls chuckled. They, too, were proud of their uncle!

"Did you get a confession from Bengler?" Jean asked.

The officer shook his head. "No, he refuses to talk."

Soon both cars had reached headquarters and the two girls hurried inside. They hugged Uncle Ned and told him how relieved they were that he was all right.

"We were worried sick over you," said Louise. "And now poor Aunt Harriet is too, because I called up to see if she had heard from you. I'll phone and tell her you're all right."

Captain Dana agreed. "Aye, you'd better do that."

This took only a few minutes, then the Danas were escorted into Captain Murphy's office. He said Bengler was in a cell but would be brought out for further interrogation.

"Before we make a definite charge against Bengler for having stolen property," said the captain, "I think the owner of these securities should come here and identify them."

Louise called Judy Platt and told her the good news. The girl was overjoyed. "Oh, you and Jean are simply marvelous!" she exclaimed.

When Judy heard of the captain's request that she identify the securities, she said, "That will be easy. They not only have my name on them, as you know, but I have a list of the serial numbers. I'll get the notebook they're in and bring it to headquarters with me."

"Fine. We'll drive over and pick you up. Are you packed so you can bring your suitcase along?"

"Yes. I'll be ready to leave in ten minutes." Judy was waiting outside when Louise and Jean pulled up at the apartment house. On the way back to headquarters, the Danas told their friend all the details of what had happened that afternoon.

"What a story!" Judy exclaimed.

In Captain Murphy's office she showed him her driver's license for identification and gave him the numbers on the stolen Master Mining stock certificates.

"These certainly match," he said, "but I judge you must have sold some of your holdings, Miss Platt."

"No, I haven't. I was waiting for the market value of them to go up."

"Well, according to your list, a hundred shares are missing!"

"Oh, no!" Judy wailed.

Jean cried out, "Then Throaty took the hundred shares with him!"

Captain Murphy looked grim. "And by this time he has probably sold them. I understand the stock is worth more now than it was a few days ago."

"That's right," Judy answered. "A hundred

shares, at the present market value, are worth twenty-five hundred dollars!"

Louise and Jean immediately thought of the item they had seen in the New York newspaper that Master Mining might rise in value. If Judy's stolen shares were not recovered, she would stand a great loss!

The officer suggested that Throaty might be traced by the police through any new purchasers.

"I doubt that's possible," Captain Dana replied. "We believe that Throaty is too clever for that. He'd know he couldn't get away with selling the securities through normal channels. What he probably did—and I feel sorry for the poor people who bought the stock—was to forge Judy Platt's name and sell the shares in small lots to unsuspecting buyers."

"That's probably right," the officer agreed. "I notice from this list that the one hundred shares are in lots of two to ten."

Captain Murphy asked a sergeant to bring Bengler from his cell. When the prisoner arrived, he was advised of his right to remain silent and to be represented by a lawyer. Bengler said this was not necessary as he was innocent.

"Bengler," said the officer, "Miss Platt has identified her stolen securities, but one hundred shares are missing. Where are they?" he demanded.

For a few moments the prisoner said nothing, then finally he muttered, "I don't know. I don't know nothin'!"

"None of that!" the police captain said sternly. "We want the truth. You know it and we're going to get it!"

"I am tellin' you the truth," Bengler insisted. "I didn't steal them papers, and I didn't have any idea they was hid under the cushion of my chair."

"Then how did they get there?" Captain Murphy asked.

Bengler shrugged. "How should I know? I suppose the thief sneaked into my apartment and put 'em there."

The officer looked scornful. "A likely story. Bengler, we might believe you, except for the fact that we know Throaty Sensky stole those certificates and you're a friend of his! What proof have you that you're not in league with him?"

The prisoner hung his head. "Sure, Throaty's a pal of mine but that don't prove *I'm* a thief."

Louise and Jean exchanged glances. They had a feeling that Captain Murphy was not going to learn the truth from his prisoner.

The captain went on, "Bengler, if you'll tell us where Throaty is, it will go easier for you when we find him."

Bengler shifted uneasily in his seat. He twisted his hands nervously, then ran them through his hair and down the sides of his face. He stood up and paced back and forth, apparently wrestling with the problem of whether or not he should reveal what he knew of Throaty's whereabouts.

Finally he made up his mind. He faced Captain Murphy and burst out, "I ain't got nothin' more to say!"

The others in the room were disappointed. Their only hope was that after spending some time in jail as a suspected accomplice, Bengler might change his mind. The sergeant was summoned and the prisoner taken away.

Captain Murphy turned to Judy. "I'm sorry, Miss Platt. I hoped Bengler would help us clear up the mystery. But don't be discouraged. After a stay behind bars—I'm sure he won't be able to raise bail money—he may decide to talk."

Judy managed to smile. "Anyway, I'm glad to recover the rest of my certificates. And thank you very much, Captain Murphy." She now turned to the Danas. "You three have been perfectly wonderful. I don't know how I can ever repay you."

To Uncle Ned's surprise, she walked over to him and planted a kiss on one cheek. "You're a dear!" she said.

Uncle Ned looked embarrassed, but he smiled and patted the girl affectionately on one shoulder.

"I haven't had a chance for a good chase on land for a long time." He chuckled. "Thank you for giving me the opportunity to try a practice sprint!"

He and the girls said good-by to Captain Murphy, who praised the Danas for their work. Then the foursome went out to the car and Uncle Ned drove home. Jean and Louise noticed that only the front porch and the hall lights were on.

"Aunt Harriet must be sitting in the dark," Jean remarked, puzzled. "I'm sure she wouldn't have gone out."

Uncle Ned stopped in front of the house. "Louise and Jean," he said, "I think it would be nicer for you to take our guest inside through the front door instead of the kitchen or the side door."

The sisters did not question him, although it went through their minds that this seemed like an unusual remark. On Judy's first visit she had come to the front door. Now she seemed like an old friend. Why hadn't their uncle gone into the driveway and let the girls off there?

Judy took her suitcase and followed the sisters up the walk. The door was opened by Aunt Harriet, who greeted Judy warmly.

"I'm glad to be here," the visitor said, smiling.

As the girls stepped into the hall, a light suddenly went on in the living room. Three male voices cried out:

"Surprise!"

CHAPTER XI

Broken Date

THE unexpected visitors at the Dana home proved to be Ken Scott, a special friend of Louise's, Chris Barton, who dated Jean, and a chum of theirs, Chuck Young.

"Ken!" Louise exclaimed to the tall, handsome blond youth, while Jean and dark-haired, good-looking Chris exchanged big grins.

The Danas introduced their friends to Judy, who liked them all, especially handsome Chuck Young. He was a well-built youth, had bright blue smiling eyes and a shock of blond hair, and looked older than his eighteen years.

The three boys attended Walton Academy, which was not far from Starhurst School. Ken and Chris frequently escorted the Danas to dances and other affairs held by the two schools.

"We phoned," said Chris, "while you girls were

out. Your aunt told us you're going away, so we thought we'd at least come over and say good-by."

Ken added, "Miss Dana has invited us to stay to dinner."

"Marvelous!" said Jean. "Oh, we have heaps of things to tell you! We'll take off our coats and be right with you."

The three girls hurried upstairs. When they returned to the first floor, Aunt Harriet announced that dinner was ready.

After they all had sat down and Captain Dana had said grace, Louise turned to her uncle.

"You knew the boys were coming," she said, smiling. "That's why you let us off at the front door. How did you find out?"

Uncle Ned's eyes twinkled. "Aunt Harriet sent a little bird who whispered it to me by way of Captain Murphy. We thought we'd let it be a surprise."

Chuck smiled. "Everything here is a big surprise to me. If it's not giving away any secrets, please tell me what this new case is you detectives are working on."

Louise laughed. "I hate to brag, but actually Jean and I are working on two cases. They both concern Judy."

She told about the stolen securities and how a hundred shares were still missing. Then Jean launched into the story of Judy's inheritance of a silver dolphin.

"And you didn't tell us!" Chris teased. "I could use a little reward money myself. How about you fellows?"

"We sure could," they said, grinning.

Jean giggled. "My mistake. If you boys had the case, I just know it would have been solved day before yesterday!"

Chuck was greatly intrigued. "And you have no idea what kind of silver dolphin you girls are looking for?"

"Not yet," Judy said. "But the reason we're going to Florida tomorrow is to see if maybe it's a live one."

The three boys whistled, and Ken asked, "If it is, what in the world are you going to do with it?"

Judy replied impishly, "I'll probably take it back to Webster with me and train it. Then I'll give exhibitions in the college swimming pool and charge admission. Anyone want to apply for the job of keeper?"

Everyone laughed, but after the hilarity had died down, Chuck said that the summer before he had been on a dig in Greece for artifacts and had found a dolphin figure.

"I felt pretty smart bringing up an ancient cup. It had the design of a dolphin on one side."

"How interesting!" said Aunt Harriet. "Tell us some more about your discovery."

"Unfortunately I couldn't keep it," said Chuck. "Against the law, you know. Right now, the cup is in a museum in Athens. Scientists dated it about 100 B.C."

"It must have been thrilling," Louise remarked.

Captain Dana asked Chuck if he had found any other artifacts.

"Only pieces of pottery, but I could see that several had the dolphin design. These sea mammals were usually shown frolicking around Greek ships. There's one piece of that kind in the museum that dates back to 540 B.C."

Chuck went on to say that while over there he had learned that the earliest known paintings of dolphins had been in 1600 B.C. This was in Tiryns, a Peloponnesian city.

"Good night!" Jean burst out. "That's really a long time ago."

The young man, enthusiastic about the subject, went on to say he had done a lot of reading of myths about dolphins and their humanlike qualities. "There's an interesting story about an escape and a rescue."

As Chuck paused, Jean said, "Oh, don't leave us in suspense! What's the story? I'm dying to hear it."

Chuck smiled. "You probably are familiar with the name Arion in connection with music. In ancient times he was considered the finest lyre player alive. He became very rich, and once, when he set sail for Corinth, the crew planned to seize his money and then throw him overboard.

"Arion begged them to let him play his lyre just once more before he drowned and they finally consented. Taking his instrument, Arion walked to the quarter-deck and played beautiful music for a long time. Dolphins, attracted by the sweet sounds, gathered around the ship. Suddenly Arion leaped overboard. One of the dolphins carried him to shore safely and he still had his money!"

"What a clever man!" Louise put in. "But what about the dolphins' humanlike traits?"

With a grin Chuck continued, "According to another legend, dolphins are human in origin. This story also takes place on a ship. When Dionysus, a Greek god traveling to Naxos, sensed that the pirate crew intended to hurl him overboard, he had his companions play lively music, and the pirates began to dance wildly. Finally, in their frenzy, they threw themselves overboard and were changed into dolphins!"

Jean laughed. "You'd think from the legend that dolphins would be wicked instead of good sea creatures!"

Chris had an answer. "Maybe the men's ducking in the ocean reformed them, especially if they couldn't swim!"

As the Danas and their guests were leaving the

table, the phone rang. Louise answered. To her amazement, the caller was Maria Castone.

"You wanted to know where Throaty Sensky is," the fortune-teller stated. "Well, he's coming here. If you still want to talk to him, drive down to my place."

"We'll be there," Louise declared.

She hung up and excitedly relayed the news to the others. Captain Dana said he hoped Maria was not up to some trick. He consented to his nieces' going, provided that the other young people went too.

"We'll go in my car," Chris said promptly.

The fortune-teller was rather surprised to see so many visitors, but she made no comment and ushered them into the back room. Maria withdrew to the front room, and the boys and girls sat in expectant silence waiting for Throaty to arrive.

Ken was restless. "Maybe I should have my palm read," he murmured.

Louise whispered, "We think she's a fake!"

Time passed. No one came in to the fortune-teller's studio. Finally Louise and Jean were convinced that the whole business was a hoax.

At ten o'clock Maria returned to the rear room and announced that she was closing her shop. "I don't know why Throaty didn't show up. He phoned me that he was coming here at nine o'clock."

The young people arose, but before leaving, Louise asked Maria, "Just why did you send for my sister and me?"

"For two reasons," the fortune-teller answered with a scowl. "First, if Throaty had come, you could have captured him. You say he's wanted by the police. Then he shouldn't be roaming around. He should be in jail." The woman shrugged. "If he didn't come, I could foresee trouble for you Danas from him tonight. I wanted to protect you."

Louise and Jean were startled by both statements.

"That was very kind of you, Miss Castone," Louise went on, "but why would you want to protect us when you placed an unlucky sign on my sister and me?"

The fortune-teller's attitude abruptly changed. She stamped her foot and shrieked, "You are very ungrateful. My reason for putting a sign on you is personal. *I* want that reward for the silver dolphin and you're not going to take it away from me!"

Maria would say no more, other than a curt good-by. The six teen-agers went outside.

"What a woman!" said Ken. "Let's go dancing for a change from that stuffy, phony place! And I could go for a nice tall soda!"

The others were enthusiastic about this idea and discussed where they would go. Several places were mentioned but did not appeal to the group. It was finally decided to try a new restaurant which had a fine dance orchestra. It was not far from Oak Falls and was called Acorn Acres.

When they reached the restaurant, Jean excused herself to telephone the Dana house to let her aunt and uncle know where they were. She made the call from a pay booth in the lobby. In a few seconds Cora Appel answered.

"Hello, Cora," said Jean. "I'd like to speak to Aunt Harriet."

"Oh, is this you, Jean?" the maid cried out. "Thank goodness you called! Somethin' dreadful has happened here. You've got to come right home!"

CHAPTER XII

Window Escape

JEAN's first impulse was to rush home at once. Then she recalled that Applecore was inclined to exaggerate and become frightened easily. Maybe the situation was not so bad after all. But if it were, Jean wanted to know at once what had happened.

"Cora," she said, "please ask Aunt Harriet to come to the phone."

The maid sighed and went off to get Miss Dana. It was at least half a minute before she arrived. Aunt Harriet's voice sounded shaky. "This time Cora is right," she said.

"Oh, dear! What happened?" Jean asked quickly.

"While your uncle was out and Cora and I were busy in the kitchen," said Aunt Harriet, "a man got into the house. I caught him in your bedroom, going through the bureau drawers. And your suitcases have been rifled, too."

"How awful! Who was the man?" Jean cried out.

"I don't know," her aunt replied. "He had his back to me. I was so frightened I screamed and of course that alerted him. He slipped out the window onto the porch roof and slid down the column."

"You didn't see his face?"

Miss Dana said the room was dark. The intruder was using a flashlight.

"Did you call the police, Aunt Harriet?"

"Yes, I did, but of course the intruder had had plenty of time to escape. The police were here and took fingerprints, though, so maybe they'll be able to identify this awful person."

"Is Uncle Ned there?" Jean asked.

"No, he won't be back for another couple of hours."

"Then we're coming right home," Jean insisted.

Miss Dana protested feebly, but Jean could tell that her aunt was still badly shaken.

"We'll be there as soon as we can make it," Jean assured her.

By the time she joined the group, they had already ordered refreshments. But when Jean told what had happened, they instantly agreed that all of them should return at once to the Dana house.

In a few minutes they were in Chris's car headed for the far side of Oak Falls. When they arrived, Cora opened the door. "Am I ever glad to see you!"

she burst out. "Think of me bein' in the kitchen washin' dishes and that man sneakin' in through a front window and goin' upstairs. Ugh! It still makes me feel sick to think about it. I guess I'm the one that left the window unlocked." Cora began to snivel.

"Don't cry," Louise said gently.

"I don't blame you for feeling nervous," said Judy. "It reminds me of Throaty breaking into my apartment. It does give one the creeps having some stranger prowling around."

Not even taking time to remove their coats, the young people trooped upstairs. Louise and Jean led the way to their bedroom. Everyone gasped in dismay at the shambles. Everything had been tossed out of the sisters' suitcases and the contents of bureaus and a desk had either been spilled onto the floor or pushed aside.

"Boy, what a mess!" Chris exclaimed. "What in the world was that guy after?"

"I'm sure it had something to do with our trip," said Louise. "Otherwise, he wouldn't have bothered searching our luggage, too."

At this, Judy flew to the room she was to occupy. Her bag had not been touched.

Meanwhile, Aunt Harriet was saying to her nieces, "Can you tell if anything is missing?"

Louise and Jean looked through their possessions. Finally they both said that nothing seemed to be gone.

"If some of our jewelry were stolen, I'd say the intruder was an ordinary burglar," Jean stated. "But I believe Louise is right—whatever he hoped to find is connected with our trip."

"Maybe," Louise said to her aunt, "you surprised him before he finished searching."

Just then the telephone rang and Aunt Harriet went to answer it. A few minutes later she came back, a grave expression on her face.

"That was the police. Our burglar was Throaty Sensky!" she announced.

"He was!" Louise exclaimed. "Now I have a theory about why he was here."

She went on to say that if Throaty were a friend of Maria Castone, possibly they were in league to try getting the reward for finding the silver dolphin. "Maria decoyed us down to her studio to give Throaty a chance to sneak into the house."

"I'm sure you're right again," Jean agreed. "Throaty was looking for some clue to where we're going—or how—plane, train, or boat tickets, or a map, or even a letter from someone."

Judy had sat down on Louise's bed and buried her face in her hands. Louise dropped beside her and asked, "Don't you feel well?"

"Physically I'm all right," Judy replied. She raised her head and Louise saw tears in the girl's eyes. "But I feel that everything that has happened is my fault. I'm responsible for all the trouble you've been put to."

Louise slipped an arm around the girl's shoulders. "For goodness' sake, Judy, you aren't to blame for anything. Jean and I didn't have to take on this mystery, and we've never worked on one yet where we didn't get into trouble. Come now, cheer up! Since Throaty didn't get a thing, why think any more about it? Let's go downstairs and have our Acorn Acres fun right here!"

"That's a great idea," said Chuck. "Come on, fellows. We'll get the stereo going and really have a ball."

Judy dried her eyes and gave a flashing smile. "I'm so lucky to have five such swell new friends," she said. "You all make me feel wonderful."

As Jean hurriedly repacked their suitcases and straightened the room, Louise decided to telephone Maria Castone to see what she would say when told the police had identified Throaty as the intruder. But the fortune-teller did not answer.

Louise shrugged. "She probably wouldn't have told me anything helpful, anyway."

The two sisters joined their friends in the living room. Uncle Ned came in and was amazed to learn what had happened during his absence.

"I'll certainly follow this up while you're gone," he declared. Then the captain said good night and went upstairs.

The rest of the evening proved to be fun for the young people. The Danas had some new dance records, and the midnight snack prepared by the three boys was delicious.

"In your spare time you ought to hire out as a chef," Jean teased Chris. "I've never eaten better cheese dreams."

Chris laughed. "I hope they won't make you dream—unless you dream about me!"

"Listen, my friend," Jean retorted teasingly, "I need a good night's sleep. Remember, we're taking a long journey tomorrow."

"How could I forget?" said Chris. "By the way, we fellows are going on a trip too—a glee club tour. The announcement was sprung on us just before we left school for the holidays."

Ken spoke up. "Too bad it doesn't include Florida. Well, I suppose we have to get going. We're staying at Chuck's house and that's quite a drive from here."

The boys got their coats, wished the girls luck in finding the silver dolphin, and said good-by.

The following morning Louise and Jean found it a little difficult to get up. Aunt Harriet had to call them twice. She finally said, "If you girls don't hurry, you'll miss your plane to New York. You can nap while you're in the air!"

Their aunt's good humor succeeded in arousing the sisters. They in turn went to waken Judy and within half an hour the Danas and their guest were eating breakfast.

When it was time to bid one another good-by, Cora began to sniff. "Oh, I wish you weren't going," she said. "Down in Florida they have hurricanes and big spiders and—"

The girls began to laugh. "What's the matter with a nice old spider?" Jean asked. Then suddenly she thought of the scorpions. Cora would be terrified if she ever heard of that episode!

"And don't get drowned!" Cora warned.

"My goodness," said Aunt Harriet, "anybody would think you were a fortune-teller, Cora. I suggest you just say good-by and happy landings, and get to work on the breakfast dishes."

Cora, still looking unhappy, did as she was told. The three girls kissed Aunt Harriet good-by, and Judy thanked Miss Dana for her hospitality. Then they climbed into the car with Uncle Ned, who headed for the airport.

"I'll be expecting success on your part," he said with a twinkle in his eyes as they went through the gate.

The flight south proved to be very pleasant the entire way. It was late afternoon when the Dana girls and Judy arrived at Miami Airport.

"Isn't this balmy air divine?" Judy exclaimed as they left the plane.

Attractive Anne Erskine was on hand to meet them. In contrast to Judy, she was shorter, a brunette, and of a more serious temperament. She had long eyelashes and naturally curly hair. After she and Judy had embraced, Judy introduced the Danas, who liked her at once.

"This is the most marvelous thing that could have happened on my vacation!" Anne said.

"And to us, too," Louise replied.

Judy laughed and said, "You Danas had better watch your step. Anne's a brain!"

Anne gave her roommate a sideways glance. "Louise and Jean, don't be misled. I get along all right studywise, but I have no detective instincts. I think your ability to solve mysteries is fantastic. I'd exchange a whole year of English poetry for a chance to catch a criminal!"

The Danas laughed as Anne led the way to her car. Reaching the street, Judy exclaimed, "Palm trees!"

"We have lots of them," Anne said. "These are coconut palms. They have been bent by the wind."

Soon the girls were rolling along an expressway. Presently Anne turned into beautiful Biscayne Bay Boulevard which ran beside a park next to the bay. "These are royal palms," she said, pointing to the tall, straight trees which lined the way.

"The trunks are encased in concrete," Louise remarked, surprised.

"That's not concrete." Anne chuckled. "It's just smooth gray bark."

She drove into a street with a wide strip of trees running down the center, then swung into the driveway of a Spanish-style house with a gleaming white tile roof.

The front door opened and Mrs. Erskine, an attractive, blond-haired woman, welcomed the visitors warmly.

As she led them into a hallway, a handsome, middle-aged man appeared from the living room at the side. Quickly Anne introduced her father.

Then she said, "I'm so excited about the Danas' mystery. I can't wait to see what will happen next."

"Something has happened already," said Mr. Erskine. "You Danas are to call home at once. I understand from your aunt that a new clue has come up in the case."

CHAPTER XIII

Frisky Dolphin

LOUISE dashed to the telephone and put in a call. Presently Captain Dana answered.

"Hello, Uncle Ned," she said. "We arrived here safely. The Erskines gave us your message about a new clue. What is it?"

"A very important one and I warn you girls to watch your step," her uncle said. "The police told me Bengler finally talked and said that Throaty had sent him word that he and another man were on their way to Miami!"

Louise groaned. "Throaty did find out we were coming here!" she cried out. "If he spies on us, he'll certainly hamper our work on the case."

Captain Dana agreed. "Try to stay out of his way," he advised.

"But how?" Louise asked. "He has the advantage! He can shadow us, and we have no idea where he may turn up here."

"Aye, that's right, my hearty," Uncle Ned agreed. "Well, I thought I'd better tell you. Keep your eyes open."

"We'll do our best," Louise promised.

The news had sobered her considerably. When she told the others about it, there was much speculation. Why was Throaty coming to Miami? Had Maria Castone given him a clue that the silver dolphin might be here? How had Throaty learned of the girls' destination? Had he perhaps overheard Aunt Harriet talking to Cora after he had sneaked into the house?

"At any rate, I'm sure he doesn't know exactly where we are staying," Jean said. "So if we can only fool him, we could throw him off our track while we're sleuthing."

Mrs. Erskine remarked that Throaty would probably begin his hunt by visiting the places Louise and Jean would most likely sleuth for a clue to the dolphin.

"And of course one of those is the Seaquarium here—the very place we must go to first of all!" Jean remarked.

Anne's father had a suggestion. "Why don't you girls visit it at an off hour? I know the manager. I'll call him and explain."

Judy suddenly began to giggle. "I have another suggestion. Louise and Jean could masquerade as boys, and be escorts for Anne and me!"

The others laughed, but Louise said, "I wonder if it would work."

Judy said she thought it was worth a try. "But you'd have to cut your hair short. Do you mind?"

Louise and Jean looked at each other, then grinned. "If it will help solve this mystery," Jean said with a smile, "I'll be glad to part with a lot of my hair!"

"Perhaps you won't have to," Louise remarked. "We could use wigs."

Anne Erskine thought the scheme a good one. "I know a place where you can buy them," she said. "But you pale-faced Northerners had better get tanned to look like us natives. That'll help your disguise, too. We have a sun lamp. With a generous amount of oil on you, it'll give you a good start on a nice cocoa shade."

After dinner Anne drove the girls to a costume store where the Danas tried on wigs. Louise selected a blond wig, and Jean took a brunette one. Then they hurried home for their sun-lamp treatments. When the Danas emerged, their faces, necks, chests, arms, and backs were evenly tanned.

"You look great!" Judy declared.

Meanwhile, Mr. Erskine had gone off to borrow some boys' clothes from a friend's college-age son. When he returned, Louise and Jean put on the shirts, slacks, and shoes, then added the wigs.

"The clothes aren't too bad a fit—just a bit loose—but I can't keep these shoes on—they're so big!" Jean complained.

"Same problem here." Louise took a step and almost tripped.

"Oh, I'll fix that," said Anne.

She went for some cotton and stuffed wads of it into the toes of the boy's shoes. "Okay?" she asked. "Will they stay on now?"

Both Louise and Jean wiggled their feet and tried walking. "I still feel clumsy, but guess I can manage," said Jean, and her sister agreed.

The four girls went into the living room where Mr. and Mrs. Erskine were watching television. The couple glanced up, then amazement came into their eyes upon seeing the disguised Danas.

Mrs. Erskine exclaimed, "I'd never recognize you two girls for the same ones who arrived here a few hours ago!"

Her husband remarked, "Better get rid of that smooth-shaven look. Add a little dirt. Otherwise, you look great."

"I'll take my big straw beach bag along," said Anne. "We'll pack it with towels, a camera, and extra clothes—in case you Danas want to look like girls again."

In the morning Anne put the bulging bag in the car and drove off with Judy and their two "escorts."

As they rode along, Jean said, "I'd like to try out

this disguise. Is there a shop we can go into?"

"Good idea," said Anne. She turned into a side street and after several blocks stopped in front of a novelty store. The Danas got out and took giant strides as they went into the shop.

On a counter lay a tray of ornaments which were shaped like dolphins. Jean picked out a gray plastic one. She went up to the man clerk and asked in a deep voice, "How much is this?"

"A dollar each, sir," was the reply.

Jean suppressed a smile and paid for the toy.

Meanwhile, Louise had selected a box of chocolate-covered coconut patties. The man addressed her as "sir" also.

Outside, the sisters broke into grins and hastened to the car.

"It worked!" Jean announced elatedly. "Now let's hope we fool Throaty if he's around!"

Anne drove eastward. As they drove over a long causeway with sparkling blue water on either side, they saw a big brown pelican dive for a fish.

"Wow!" Jean exclaimed.

"This is part of Biscayne Bay," Anne explained. "The Seaquarium is on an island called Virginia Key."

When they reached the Seaquarium, Anne introduced herself to the man at the gate. He picked up a telephone and called the manager, who arrived in a few minutes. He looked surprised to see two boys, but Anne whispered the secret to him.

He laughed and led the girls down a walk past a garden of red and purple flowers. At the end stood a large blue building. The visitors followed the man into a dimly lighted circular corridor which, he explained, curved around the main tank.

Through big windows the girls could see a weird underwater scene. Amid the fish swam a giant turtle and many dolphins, including a few babies.

"These dolphins are really bottle-nosed porpoises," the manager remarked.

Suddenly Judy gave a little cry. "Ugh! Look at this creature!"

Close to the glass lurked a long, cylindrical snakelike fish with a round ugly head.

"That's a moray eel," said their guide. "They like to hide in the rocks and dart out to bite our divers when the men go in to feed the fish."

Judy shuddered.

"There are other dangerous creatures in here, too," he added. "The sawfish and the ray, for instance."

When the visitors reached a stairway, the manager said, "Go up and watch the fun. A dolphin is being put through her tricks. Afterward, we'll talk about your mystery. You'll find me in our garden restaurant."

The girls thanked him and walked up the steps and over to the rail at the edge of the main tank, into which they had been looking downstairs. At one side, extending over the water, was a high platform which was shaped like the prow of a boat. On it stood a young man in white slacks. He held a fish high in the air and talked to a dolphin frolicking in the water.

"Come on there, Dolly, dance on your tail!" the trainer ordered.

The dolphin squealed and dived. She came up, stood upright on her tail, and scooted swiftly backward across the water. At the same time, the trainer flung the fish which she caught while "dancing." Then she dived again.

The four girls clapped at the delightful performance. At once Dolly was attracted to the sound and streaked to where they were standing. As the dolphin came closer, she squealed loudly.

"Dolly wants us to give her a fish," Judy said, laughing.

A sudden idea came to Jean. She leaned far over the railing and extended the plastic fish as a teaser, which she did not intend the frisky dolphin to swallow.

But Dolly leaped up and caught the toy fish in her teeth. Jean held on. The next second the dolphin dropped back into the tank, yanking Jean headlong into the water!

Her friends screamed and Louise cried, "She'll be bitten by that eel!"

The trainer hurried down from his perch to the

side of the pool. The dolphin by now was circling around the floating plastic fish and playing with it.

Jean had come to the surface and now swam frantically to the edge of the tank. "Hurry! Hurry!" the other girls urged.

The trainer leaned down and with a heave pulled the frightened girl out of the water.

"Oh, thank you!" Jean gasped.

After she had assured them all she was unharmed, the trainer grinned and said, "I think I'll add that trick to Dolly's act." The handsome young man winked. "You want to apply?"

"No, thanks," said Jean in her normal voice.

The man laughed. "So you're a girl! What is this? Halloween?"

Jean was cross with herself and exasperated, but she was always a good sport when being teased. "I'm sorry I can't explain. Right now, I'd like to go and dry off."

Taking the beach bag, she hurried downstairs to a ladies' rest room.

"This is good-by to my disguise," Jean thought as she quickly changed into yellow shorts and a shirt.

When she was ready, all the girls went to the restaurant in the rear of the building. They found the manager talking to a gardener who was trimming a high hedge of pink hibiscus.

The playful dolphin yanked Jean into the water

The manager waved the girls to a table in the shade of a tree and called an order to a waiter inside the building. In a few minutes they were all sipping ice-cold lemonade and telling their story.

Then the manager in turn informed them that a few years ago Oliver Platt had come to see him. "He asked me if I knew any captain with a boat and equipment for catching dolphins."

"That was my brother!" Judy cried out. "What else did he say?"

The manager recalled that Mr. Platt had not stated the reason for his request.

"I recommended Captain Grand. He was often engaged by people to take them out and bring in sea mammals. The captain had a very fine boat, called the *Triton*. It had a large tank, and a strong net for snaring dolphins and hoisting them aboard. You have to be very careful when capturing a dolphin because if it is injured when it is brought aboard, the creature may die. In fact, when ours travel, we put foam-rubber mattresses in their boxes."

"Where is Captain Grand now?" Judy asked, feeling that a big stride had been made in solving the mystery.

"I have no idea," was the disappointing answer. "I asked for him one time, but learned he never returned from the trip he made, presumably with Mr. Platt as his passenger."

"Never returned? You mean something happened to him?" Judy asked fearfully.

"I wouldn't say that," the manager replied. "If he had been in trouble while at sea, he would have radioed for help, but no such message ever came through."

"Then where *is* Captain Grand?" Louise asked, completely puzzled.

CHAPTER XIV

The Seaman's Clue

THE manager of the Seaquarium shook his head and looked at Judy sympathetically. "I wish I could help you. Finding this silver dolphin means a great deal to you, doesn't it?"

"Yes, it's my inheritance from my brother."

"I see," said Mr. Ackerman. "I'm sorry I haven't some good clue for you. But here's a suggestion. Why don't you all go to the dock where Captain Grand used to keep his boat? Maybe someone there can give you information about him or the *Triton*."

The Danas thought this was an excellent idea, and listened carefully to his directions.

"The dock won't be easy to find," he warned. "There are so many waterways and keys around this area only a real native can find his way around."

"I live here," said Anne, "so it shouldn't be too hard. Can we get there by car?"

"Yes, but you'll have to walk a distance after you park."

As they went out the front gate, early visitors were arriving, and a number of cars were parked outside. The Danas and their friends hurried to their own automobile. Soon Anne was heading south, down the highway to Key Largo.

In about an hour she pulled up in front of a strip of stores beside the road. One of them was marked "Alligator Jack's Restaurant."

"That's the sign the manager told us to look for," Anne said.

The girls got out of the car and walked down a sandy side road toward the waterfront. There were a few houses along the way with chickens running loose in the yards and blue morning glories climbing up the bleached wooden fences. At last the girls came to a wide beach and a long dock.

Seated under an awning outside a building marked "Office," they found the dockmaster. He said he had known Captain Grand well. Judy told him she wanted to talk with the captain. "Where is he?"

"I don't know, miss. Last time I saw Captain Grand he didn't say where he was headin' or for how long. He had one crewman with him on the *Triton* and one passenger. But I think he was goin' to pick up a second crewman at another dock."

"What did the passenger look like?" Judy inquired.

After the man had described him, she turned to her friends. "That was Oliver, all right." Impulsively she asked the dockmaster, "Did you ever hear this passenger or Captain Grand or the crewman mention a silver dolphin?"

The man shook his head. "Silver dolphin? What kind would such a critter be?"

"That's just the trouble," said Anne. "We don't know."

Louise had remained silent on purpose. She wanted the dockmaster to think that she was a boy. But now, since Judy showed great disappointment and seemed willing to leave, Louise finally spoke up in as deep a voice as she could muster. "Do you know about a constellation called the dolphin?"

The dockmaster became thoughtful. At last he replied, "I've only heard of it, but I do remember Captain Grand and his passenger talkin' about a dolphin constellation."

"What did they say?" Jean inquired.

The man scratched his head. "Seems to me they were arguin' about how many stars are in the constellation. Sure—it comes back to me now. The passenger insisted that when you're down in the Caribbean, you can see only four stars with the naked eye and on a clear night at that. Captain Grand said the navigational charts show five bright stars."

Grinning, the dockmaster went on, "Some time later, when I took an astronomy guy out in a boat, I asked him how many stars there were in the dolphin. And what do you think? He told me six! He said you could see them easy through binoculars and there are even more than that in the whole constellation, but you can only see them with a telescope."

The four girls had been hanging on the man's words. There must be a real link with the mystery in this clue of Oliver Platt's interest in Delphinus.

Unaware of their excitement, the dockmaster said with a chuckle, "Well, one thing's sure. I ain't never goin' to get to visit any of those dolphin stars. But I don't care. I'm satisfied to stay down here on earth. Let other folks hunt for dolphins in the sky!"

The girls laughed. Then Jean asked him, "How long ago did Captain Grand and his one passenger leave here?"

"Oh, it was over a year ago."

Louise turned to Judy. "Does that fit in with what you know?"

The girl nodded. "The last time I saw my brother alive was a little over a year ago—at Thanksgiving time."

Anne noticed that the man had a wire basket of fresh fish hanging from one side of the dock. She asked if they were for sale.

"Sure. You like pompano?"

"Love 'em," Anne said with a laugh. "I'll buy a couple."

The man brought up the basket and she made her selection. He had nothing in which to wrap them, however, so Anne was forced to carry the two fish in her hands. As the girls reached the car, she said, "Will somebody please unlock the trunk and get out a few sheets of the newspaper in there?"

Louise did so and the fish were quickly wrapped. Then Anne wiped her hands as well as she could on more newspaper. She grimaced. "I hate to get the wheel all fishy. Will one of you girls drive?"

Judy volunteered, and her roommate gave directions on how to get back home. Mrs. Erskine was delighted to have fresh fish and said she would cook the pompano for lunch.

It proved to be delicious, but Judy ate little. From her sad expression, the others could tell that she was discouraged about her inheritance. As they left the table, she said, "Where do we go from here in our sleuthing?"

Jean had a suggestion. "Surely Captain Grand has relatives or close friends around here. If we could find out who they are, maybe one of them could help us."

Judy's face brightened and her enthusiasm returned. Mr. Erskine said he would try to find out through a seaman's club about any friends or family of Captain Grand. A little later he reported success. The captain had a cousin who was a retired seaman named Wally Wallace.

"He lives in a little house along the beach on Plantation Key," Mr. Erskine reported. "Too bad you didn't know it this morning when you were near there."

He gave directions and within half an hour the girls were off to quiz Wally Wallace.

His small white stucco house stood amid a grove of palm trees and low-growing cabbage palmettos near the water. A row of large, round pieces of white coral lined a path to the door. The old man was fishing from his dock when the girls arrived.

He was very friendly and apparently ready for any audience to whom he could spin tall tales of the sea. Wally seemed to accept Louise as a young man.

He did not even ask his visitors' names and started right in by saying he supposed they had come to hear some of his stories. After he had told several humorous ones, Judy interrupted.

"I'm sorry," she said politely, "but we came here to ask about a cousin of yours, Captain Grand. We're interested in finding him."

"So that's it," the seaman said. "Well, I'm obliged to tell you that I don't know. Cousin Abner left these parts more'n a year ago in the *Triton* and nobody's heard from him since or seen his boat."

Wally gave the girls a long wink. "It's my opinion he got himself a wife and stayed wherever she lives. He was a bachelor, you know. I'll bet you he's married to a Spanish or Portuguese lass on one of the Caribbean islands."

The girls were so amazed at this suggestion that they just stared at one another and then at Wally Wallace. The old man enjoyed the startling effect of his announcement.

Chuckling again, he added, "Abner's probably out catchin' dolphins to amuse her."

For a moment the four callers had thought the story might be true, but now they felt sure Wally Wallace was merely teasing them.

Louise, speaking in a deep voice, asked the retired seaman, "Did you ever see a silver dolphin or hear of one?"

"Silver? No, sir. But I'll tell you what, lad. Once I saw a white one—an albino. They're precious rare in these waters. But a silver one? No. Is there such a thing?"

"We don't know," Louise answered.

During the latter part of the conversation, Wally had led the girls into his house. Once inside, he invited them to sit down in his living room. It was an amazing place, full of relics of the sea and foreign ports.

Louise's attention was attracted to a wall map of the Caribbean, which hung across the room. She arose to look at it.

The elderly man noticed this. "That's an old-timer," he said. "Don't go by that, though, if you want to find anythin'. That map was drawn before the Caribbean had been very well charted. I guess some of the names have even been changed."

Louise read the wording alongside each dot which represented an island. She hunched her shoulders in distaste at one. Then she suddenly realized that this was a feminine gesture, and she was supposed to be a boy!

Straightening up, she said in her disguised voice, "Here's an island called Job's Coffin. Is there a special story about it?"

Wally Wallace looked startled. "Did you say Job's Coffin?"

As Louise nodded, he went on, "My cousin Abner once visited that place. Told me it was deserted. But there was a legend that a bunch of blood-thirsty pirates once used it for a raiding base."

As the old seaman paused, it flashed through Jean's mind that if this were true, Captain Grand might have gone there looking for buried treasure with Mr. Platt!

The girls stared excitedly at one another. Louise was the first to recover from the girls' surprise and said, "They might have found a live silver-colored dolphin near Job's Coffin, and kept it there. We must find Captain Grand and ask him!"

"Well, I sure wish I could help you all more," Wally said.

Judy assured him he had given them a valuable

clue. The Danas nodded agreement. Now they did have something on which to work. The girls thanked the old seaman and started to leave. Jean paused to give him the Erskines' address in case he came across any further information for them.

Louise was the first to step out of the house. She heard someone whistle and jerked her head to the left to see who it was.

At the same instant, something rolled with lightning speed from behind a tree to her right, directly into her path. She did not see it and stumbled headlong over the object. Louise tried to catch herself, but her ill-fitting boy's shoes kept her from retaining her balance.

As Louise fell headlong to the ground, she hit her forehead hard on a big coral rock and blacked out!

CHAPTER XV

A Mysterious Island

ANNE and Judy, who had followed Louise outside, rushed to the girl's side. Jean was close behind.

Judy said quickly, "We'll take care of her, Jean. You find the person who rolled this thing."

The "thing" proved to be a stone around which a thick white bark had been wrapped but was now half off. Jean, sure that her sister was not badly hurt, but merely knocked out momentarily, looked around quickly. Seeing no one, Jean directed her gaze along the path left by the rolling stone and thought she detected a movement behind one of the palm trees.

Like a shot Jean was off. Wally Wallace had burst from the shack and joined the chase.

"Low-down sea hound!" he muttered.

When Jean reached the tree, no one was there,

but a trail of small barefoot prints indicated in which direction the stone thrower had gone. The old seaman caught up to Jean and she pointed them out.

"I'm going to follow these tracks," she told him.

"Me too," Wally said grimly.

Jean ran through the tangled scrubgrass and palm trees. Her progress was slowed because the footprints sometimes were not visible. She managed to pick them up again, with Wally close behind. The footprints led directly to a small house.

Jean and the seaman walked up and knocked. There was no answer.

"I'm sure the person is inside," said Jean. "Do you know who lives here?"

"I sure do. Name's Nuger. From the size of these footprints, I think they belong to the boy Sammy."

When repeated knocks failed to bring anyone to the door, Wally shouted, "Sammy Nuger, you come out here! We know you tossed that stone. It hurt somebody, too."

There was still no response from within and finally the old man yelled, "Sammy, if you don't come out, I'm goin' to fetch the police!"

This threat did the trick. In a few seconds the door opened to reveal a boy of about twelve years old.

"You ought to have a good thrashin'," said Wally. "Better talk fast."

Sammy hung his head. He did not speak, so Wally threatened again to bring the police.

"All—all right, I'll talk," the boy stammered.

He finally told his listeners that a man had come up to him on the beach. "The man said he'd give me some money if I did him a favor. He wanted me to throw a stone at the first person that came out of your place, Mr. Wallace."

Shamefaced, Sammy toed the sand. "I said okay and took the money. But I didn't want to hurt nobody so I wrapped the stone in punk bark."

"In what?" Jean asked.

"The bark of the punk tree," Wally Wallace explained. "It's an Oriental tree that grows around here. The Chinese grind up the bark to make punk for joss sticks and lightin' fireworks."

"It's soft," the boy put in, "and I figured the stone wouldn't hurt much that way. And I didn't throw the stone, either. I just rolled it along the sand."

"Who was the man who paid you?" Jean asked.

"I don't know—never saw him before, so I reckon he's a stranger around here."

"What does he look like?" Jean inquired.

"Oh, nothin' special. He was medium height and had black hair," Sammy replied. "The only thing

funny about him was his voice. He talked awful
hoarse. I reckon he's got a bad sore throat."

Jean "reckoned" otherwise. She was sure that the
man was Throaty Sensky!

She asked Sammy several other questions as to
where Throaty had come from or where he might
be staying, but the boy could not answer any of
them. "Throaty was very careful not to reveal
that," Jean thought.

She was also sure that the man had been spying
on the girls. Ruefully Jean concluded that her own
and Louise's boy disguises had not fooled their enemy. "It's probably my fault," she thought.
"Throaty may have spotted me from one of those
parked cars as we left the Seaquarium.

"And I'll bet he was the person who whistled to
distract Louise's attention so Sammy could throw
the stone without being seen," Jean added to herself.

Wally Wallace, meanwhile, had spared no words
in berating Sammy. The boy seemed completely
cowed and promised that never again would he take
money from a stranger, or anyone else, to hurt
another person.

To Jean's surprise, Sammy said, "I want to walk
back with you and see about your friend. I hope he
ain't hurt bad."

When the threesome returned to Wally's house
they found that Louise had soon regained con-

sciousness, and other than a bruise on her forehead, she was all right. Shyly, Sammy apologized for what he had done and said he was glad "the young man" was okay. Then he turned and ran up the beach toward his own home.

Louise's good spirits had returned. "Some people you fool and some you don't," she said.

"One that your disguise hasn't fooled is Throaty," Jean declared, then reported what Sammy had said and told of her suspicions of how Throaty Sensky had tracked down the girls.

Louise frowned. "You're right, I'm afraid, Jean. From now on I might as well wear my own clothes!"

"You won't be sorry." Jean chuckled. "And it'll feel good to get that wig off." Becoming serious again, she said, "I wonder how much Throaty has found out about what we've learned."

Louise felt sure he knew nothing as yet about the location of Job's Coffin island.

The others agreed and Wally Wallace offered to do his part by reporting the whole incident to the police. The Danas were glad to have him do this.

"Sensky is wanted by the authorities up North," Louise said. "He's a thief."

The friendly seaman promised to let the girls know if he learned anything more. "If that varmint comes sneakin' around here, I'll fix him!"

The girls thanked him, then walked to the car

and slowly drove home. On the way, they watched the rear-view mirror, but did not see any car that was deliberately following them.

"All the same, I'll bet Throaty's trailing us," Judy said nervously, "—or maybe some pal of his is following us."

"Yes," Louise agreed. "He'll find out where we're staying, all right."

Back at the Erskines', the girls learned that Anne's parents had invited an astronomer, Professor Vinson, to be their guest at dinner.

"I thought you girls might get some helpful information from him. I told him about the stars around the signature of Judy's brother," said Mrs. Erskine.

The Danas in particular were thrilled with this idea, and looked forward to obtaining another clue to the dolphin mystery. Professor Vinson arrived promptly. He was about thirty-five, and handsome. No sooner were introductions made than the professor himself brought up the subject of the mystery.

Louise told him the whole story and he was both interested and puzzled by Judy's inheritance of a silver dolphin.

"One possible clue we've picked up," Louise said, "is that Mr. Platt may have been keeping the silver dolphin at a desolate island in the Caribbean called Job's Coffin, where he once went with Captain Grand. Have you ever heard of the island?"

Professor Vinson said he had not, but added, "Job's Coffin is a nickname for the constellation Delphinus."

"It is?" the Danas cried out. Louise went on, "I'm sure now that we're on the right track!"

"Oh, I hope so," Judy spoke up. "If my brother went there, though, but didn't come back with Captain Grand, how *did* he return to the United States?"

Anne said, "Maybe he had a plane pick him up at the island."

Mr. Erskine asked, "Judy, do you think your brother had a boat of his own?"

Judy could not be positive, but doubted it. "Neither a private boat nor a plane was mentioned in Oliver's will."

Jean had a theory. "Perhaps Captain Grand did return, but landed at a port outside the Miami area. We might check with other docks along the Atlantic coast."

"But that would take too long," Anne said. "There are hundreds of them."

Her father agreed. "We'd better try some other way first."

During dinner, which ended with a Floridian special—Key lime pie—made of creamy lime-colored custard topped with meringue, conversation was animated. It was almost exclusively on the subject uppermost in everyone's mind—finding the silver dolphin.

"It's maddening!" Jean exclaimed. "We have such great clues, yet we can't seem to fit them together to learn the secret!"

At the end of the meal, Mr. Erskine offered a suggestion. "Suppose you girls get in touch with the airport and inquire about a chartered plane to the Caribbean. Perhaps you'll learn whether or not Mr. Platt had been a passenger on one of them."

"We'll do that tomorrow!" Judy cried enthusiastically. "Oh, why does there have to be a night?"

The others smiled as Louise said, "So there'll be dolphin stars for you to look at!"

Suddenly Jean leaned forward and looked straight at Mr. Erskine. "By any chance, do you have in mind that maybe *we* might charter a plane ourselves and go to Job's Coffin?"

Anne's father burst into laughter. "I wondered how soon somebody would catch on," he said.

All the girls became excited at the idea of sleuthing over the Caribbean. Louise said she and her sister would have to obtain permission from their Aunt Harriet and Uncle Ned. "And also some money," she added. "I hope, since Mr. Howell is handling Mr. Platt's estate, he'll be willing to finance our flight."

"Oh, he just has to!" Jean exclaimed.

The girls excused themselves and Louise went directly to the telephone. Before she could dial, the phone began to ring. She answered and to her amazement found that Aunt Harriet was on the wire.

"You're a mind reader!" Louise said. "I was just going to call you. Is everything all right?"

Her aunt's voice sounded somber as she said, "I've just had a warning from Maria Castone. She told me a written message had suddenly appeared on the palm of one hand and it concerns you and Jean."

"How ridiculous!" said Louise.

"Wait a minute," Aunt Harriet begged, "until you hear the message. It read:

" *'Dana girls planning trip over water. Warn them not to go. They will never return!'* "

CHAPTER XVI

Forged Signature

FOR a moment Louise was almost too stunned to respond to her aunt's news. But she quickly collected her wits. "Aunt Harriet," she said, "Jean and I *are* planning a trip across water—the Caribbean. We have a terrific lead to where the silver dolphin may be. Please say we can go! Surely you don't believe that mumbo-jumbo of Maria Castone's."

Miss Dana, however, seemed really frightened by the fortune-teller's sinister revelation, and argued, "Maybe Maria didn't actually see that message written on her hand, but she may have received some psychic warning."

Louise realized she would have to be very persuasive. "Aunt Harriet, you know that Jean and I have a strong hunch that Maria Castone and Throaty Sensky are in league. By the way, today we found out he was trailing us. I believe he has learned we plan to look for the silver dolphin on a Caribbean island and he'd undoubtedly try anything to stop us."

Louise did not tell her aunt about the man's attempt to injure her. "I'm sure," she went on, "that Throaty contacted Maria Castone and told her to give you some scary message so you'd forbid us to make the trip."

There was silence on the other end of the line and finally Louise said, "Are you still there, Aunt Harriet?"

"Yes. I'm thinking. Maybe you're right, and Maria did invent the story. I shouldn't be so quick to believe these weird things. Now, tell me more about this proposed trip."

Louise brought her aunt up to date. Miss Dana was finally convinced that it would be all right for them to go to Job's Coffin island. "Of course you'll have to convince Mr. Howell and your Uncle Ned. Wait a minute."

After Louise told Captain Dana the story and made her request, her uncle said, "I'll give my consent on one condition—that you have three strong, reliable men with you. If you don't land, they can just enjoy the ride. But if you do try sleuthing on Job's Coffin—I must admit I've never heard of it—then you'll have the men there to protect you."

Louise thanked him, then asked Uncle Ned to

give her the phone number of Mr. Howell's home. She jotted it down, said good-by to her uncle, then called the trust officer.

While Louise was waiting for him to answer, she could feel her heart pounding. Would Mr. Howell agree to advance the money for a chartered plane? Or was the girls' sleuthing going to end right now?

When he answered, she told him in detail what the girls had learned. Mr. Howell expressed amazement. "You Danas and your friends are certainly doing a topnotch job!"

Quickly Louise made her request. "All of us here feel strongly that if we fly to Job's Coffin island, we'll find the solution to the mystery."

"Hmm," said Mr. Howell. "Well, in that case, all right. Be sure to charter a safe plane."

"Oh, thanks a million! We'll let you know what happens."

When the conversation was finished, she hurried to tell the others the good news. Jean gave a war whoop and Judy squealed in delight.

"That's great!" said Anne. "And what three men are going with us?"

"I'll volunteer," said her father at once.

Young Professor Vinson smiled. "Maybe I can be of assistance. One of my avocations is flying. Besides, there may be something on Job's Coffin worth an archaeological search, which is another interest of mine."

"And, of course, the pilot will be the third man," said Louise.

Another hour was spent in talking about the Caribbean flight, then Mr. Vinson arose to depart. "From now on, please call me Prof." He chuckled. "All my friends do."

Laughingly the girls agreed, and promised to keep him posted on trip plans.

"Fine. I can be ready on fifteen minutes' notice."

The following morning Mr. Erskine said he would take Judy and Jean to a seaplane port on Biscayne Bay. Anne had chores to do for her mother. Louise, extremely fatigued from her experience the day before, said she would stay at home and rest.

Upon reaching the waterfront, Mr. Erskine and the two girls walked past a row of seaplanes to the small office building where aircraft could be chartered. They learned from the young woman clerk that Mr. Platt was not listed among the people who had ever engaged such services.

"So how he got back to the mainland is still a mystery," Judy remarked.

Next, Mr. Erskine inquired if there was a seaplane available that could be chartered. There was, the young woman said.

"We'd also like a pilot who could act as strong-arm man if necessary," Jean said.

The clerk looked up in surprise. She made no

comment, but highly recommended a pilot named Dave James.

"You'll like him," she said with a smile.

When the two girls met Dave James, they were inclined to agree. He was a very good-looking, athletic type, and beamed when he was asked if he would take on the assignment.

"I sure will," said Dave. "It sounds like a real adventure. I can have the seaplane ready by Monday. Okay?"

There was a short conference, and Monday morning was decided upon. Jean now asked Dave if he would be willing to have Professor Vinson as copilot.

"Yes, indeed," Dave replied. "I know Prof. He's an excellent pilot and a great guy to have around."

"So long until Monday then," Jean said as she and the others left.

When they pulled up in front of the Erskine house, Jean and Judy were astounded to see Wally Wallace being admitted at the front door. With a quick explanation to Mr. Erskine, the girls jumped from the car and hastened inside just as Wally was saying to Louise and Anne, "I got somethin' to show you all."

He took a folded paper from his pocket but did not hand it over. Instead, he said, "Last night a fellow came to my house. He said he'd give me

somethin' valuable in return for certain information."

"Was it Throaty Sensky?" Louise asked him
quickly, and gave the suspect's description.

"Well, he did look like that, and he did have a
hoarse voice—but he said his name was Albert
Zimmer."

"He could have been using an assumed name,"
Louise remarked.

"Yep, that's true. Anyway, I didn't feel I could
tackle him, tie him up, and call the police by myself,
so I just asked him what kind of information was he
after."

The seaman went on to say that what Mr.
Zimmer wanted to do was look at the antique map
on the wall. "I couldn't see no harm in that," Wally
said.

"When the man looked at the map," Judy spoke
up, "did he say anything to you about it?"

Wally shook his head. "Not a word. But he
pulled a paper and pencil from his pocket and
scribbled some notes."

Louise and Jean exchanged glances. They were
positive that the caller had been Throaty and he had
jotted down notations on the location of Job's
Coffin island!

The old seaman went on, "After Mr. Zimmer
finished his notes he started to go, but I asked him,
'What am I supposed to get for lettin' you have the

information?' So he pulls this paper from his pocket and gives it to me. I don't know what it's all about. I thought maybe you could tell me."

Anne asked the retired sailor why Mr. Zimmer had not explained the paper to him.

"Search me. But he did say somethin' funny when he was handin' it to me—'You look tough, Wally, so I won't argue with you about keeping my promise. I got more important things to do. Now listen. Hide this paper away. Someday it'll be worth a lot of money.'"

Wally handed the paper to Judy. She unfolded it quickly, then gasped.

"This is one of my missing stock certificates!" she cried out. Turning it over, she said, "And my signature has been forged on the SELLER's line!"

The others crowded around to look at the certificate. Wally's caller beyond a doubt must have been Throaty Sensky!

Louise explained to Wally that the document was stolen property. "I'll notify the police."

She hurried off to do this. The police officer to whom she spoke agreed that Albert Zimmer might be an alias Throaty was using in Miami. He assured Louise an immediate hunt would be undertaken for him in hotels, motels, and rooming houses.

When Louise rejoined the group, Jean was just asking Wally if he thought Throaty might have followed him to the Erskine home.

The seaman grinned. "No, ma'am. I took my

little outboard boat and came ashore near here by a special route. He couldn't know about it."

"That's good," said Jean. "But Throaty may pick up your trail when you leave and try to get information about us from you. I think you should stay here until after dark."

Mr. Erskine had come into the room and heard this part of the conversation. He said, "Wally, Jean's idea is a wise one. Suppose you come with me to my workshop. Do you like to work with tools and build things?"

The visitor chuckled. "I like it, but I never get around to it." He followed Mr. Erskine from the room.

After the men had left, Jean and Judy told about the arrangements they had made for Monday's flight to Job's Coffin.

Anne grinned. "I can't wait to see this Dave James," she said. "He sounds divine."

Louise declared, "The thought of our seaplane sleuthing has really revived me."

"Swell!" Anne said. "Just in time for a party tonight. I've invited some of my crowd to supper, and dancing later."

For a few hours that evening the girls thoroughly enjoyed themselves and put the mystery and Throaty Sensky out of their minds. Wally left about ten o'clock.

The following day the Danas attended church with their friends, then packed their bags in case they should stay at Job's Coffin or one of the neighboring tropical islands. Anne suggested they take along scuba gear. She had her own, and would borrow equipment for the Danas and Judy. Mrs. Erskine insisted that they also take a large quantity of fresh water and prepared food.

Anne chuckled. "We can always eat roots and berries, Mother, if push comes to shove."

The Danas looked puzzled. "If what?" Jean asked.

"If worst comes to worst," Anne translated. "That's how some of us Floridians say it."

Louise laughed. "Well, no roots and berries for me, thank you. I prefer Mrs. Erskine's selections!"

Later, at dusk, a call came from the police. Mr. Erskine was informed by the sergeant on duty, "We have Albert Zimmer here. Will the Danas and Miss Platt please come down and identify him?"

Louise and Jean were electrified—their enemy had been captured! Within minutes they were on their way to headquarters with Judy and Mr. Erskine.

CHAPTER XVII

Ocean Rescue

WHEN Mr. Erskine and the three girls reached headquarters, they went at once to the desk and introduced themselves. The sergeant pointed to the rear of the room and said, "That man over there calls himself Albert Zimmer. Do you recognize him?"

Louise and Jean took a look at the nervous, pale man hunched over in a chair, then suddenly dashed forward.

Jean cried out in disbelief, "Why, you're Al from the Oak Falls Pharmacy!"

"Sure I am," the man said, a look of relief coming over his face. His voice was hoarse. "And you're the Dana girls! Thank goodness you came. These people are trying to tell me I'm somebody else. And a thief at that!"

"You have a cold, haven't you?" Jean asked.

"Yes. Can't get rid of it. That's why I came South," Al replied.

The sergeant and the two officers guarding Al looked even more amazed than Mr. Erskine and Judy. "You know this man?" the sergeant asked the Danas. "Where is he from?"

"The town we live in," Louise replied. "I only knew him by his first name, Al." She turned to the drugstore clerk. "Is your last name Zimmer?"

"Yes, it is."

By this time he was standing up, and shook hands fervently with Louise and Jean. "You're the Danas who are such good detectives, aren't you?"

"We try," Louise said, smiling, then introduced Judy and Mr. Erskine. Indicating Judy, she said to Al, "The man we're looking for stole some valuable property from her. He's the one using your name."

Al's face registered shock. "A cr-crook going under my name? For Pete's sake, why pick on me?" He turned to the sergeant. "I'm not going to be held any longer, am I?"

The sergeant assured Al he was free to go. "Too bad we had to bring you to headquarters, but naturally I guess you understand why. I'll alert all our men that Sensky's using your name."

The sergeant opened a desk drawer and brought out two tickets which he handed to Zimmer with a smile. "These were sent here. They're for a big swimming meet. Maybe you'd enjoy seeing it."

"Gee, thanks," said Al. "I sure would."

He thanked the Danas again, then hurried off. The girl detectives and their friends continued to discuss this new aspect of the case. Louise and Jean felt strongly that somehow Throaty learned Al Zimmer was to be in Miami at this time and decided to appropriate his name.

"Well, he succeeded in throwing us on the wrong track for a while," Jean said dryly.

Louise had an additional thought. "I have a hunch Maria Castone is the one who gave Throaty the idea. She probably went into the Oak Falls Pharmacy and heard Al talking about his trip."

The group said good night to the sergeant, who promised to continue a search for the thief. "If he's around here, we'll pick him up," the officer assured them.

But up to the time Mr. Erskine drove the Danas, Judy, and Anne to the seaplane port the next morning, they had had no report from headquarters. Prof met them at the dock where the seaplane was moored. It was a large, sleek model. Dave James hopped from the cabin to greet his passengers and said the craft was tuned up.

"We're ready to take off as soon as I receive clearance from the tower."

"I love the name of the plane," Judy said dreamily. "*Cloud Gull*. We'll all become sea gulls and soar into the clouds!"

Her remark put everyone in a happy frame of

mind as they climbed aboard and found seats. Dave took his place at the controls with Prof beside him and awaited instructions from the tower at Miami International Airport. Finally they came and the craft slid gracefully across the water.

When they were airborne, the girls could see the blue waters of Biscayne Bay lying between the mainland and Miami Beach. Beyond its row of sky-scraper hotels were the whitecaps of the Atlantic Ocean.

Louise had made a crude map of the location of Job's Coffin island as marked on Wally Wallace's map. As Dave set off in the direction indicated, he pointed out a long island just off the coastline.

"Key Largo!" he shouted over the roar of the engine. "Largest of the Florida Keys!"

They flew on and on. Finally he announced that according to the map, they should be approaching Job's Coffin soon. But nothing resembling the spot appeared on the ocean surface.

"We'd better land at the next big island and ask directions," Dave suggested.

When they reached it, everyone went ashore and into the small village. Mr. Erskine inquired of several residents about Job's Coffin. They looked at him as if he were joking. No one had ever heard of it!

"Maybe Wally's map is strictly a decoration," Jean said, discouraged. "It looks as if our trip is turning into a wild-goose chase."

Louise was not willing to concede defeat. "Remember, Wally said the island is supposed to be uninhabited. That probably accounts for the people here not knowing it by name."

Mr. Erskine suggested that they have luncheon before resuming their flight. The simple but tasty meal revived the searchers' spirits. When they were airborne again, Dave flew in a more southeasterly direction than he had followed before.

"I have a hunch the old map was drawn for navigators, but it's off a few degrees," he said. "Anyway, I'll try the area directly ahead."

Late in the afternoon as Jean was looking through binoculars she said excitedly, "I see a tiny island—straight in front of us!"

They had flown only another half minute when Louise exclaimed, "Look! Down there! An overturned sailboat with a man clinging to it!"

Everyone stared. Louise was right!

"Oh, we must rescue him!" she urged.

The *Cloud Gull* descended, but it soon became apparent that the sea was pretty rough.

"I won't be able to get very close," Dave said, "or we'll smash into the boat and probably injure the man."

He circled, then set the craft down and taxied within three hundred feet of the boat. Louise and Jean kicked off their shoes and pulled open the door.

"We'll rescue him," Jean called out.

"Wait!" Prof cried. "I'll go!"

But Louise and Jean had already dived into the choppy water. They swam in long, even strokes toward the capsized sailboat.

When the sisters reached it, they saw that the shipwrecked man was young and apparently of Indian descent. His big brown eyes were sad, but he gave the girls a wan smile of hope.

The Danas, treading water, smiled back. Louise said, "Do you speak English?"

"Yes. I, Manu, can speak to you in English."

"Are you hurt?" Louise went on. When he shook his head, she asked, "Can you swim to the seaplane?"

"Manu is very weak. I have been here all night with no food."

"You poor thing!" said Jean. "My sister and I will help you. Where did you come from?"

"Manu must not tell. And Manu must wait for his friends to rescue him."

"Why?" Jean asked as the girls came nearer to him. "Surely you want to go home. We'll take you there in the plane." To the Danas' bewilderment, Manu clung to the boat and made no effort to move away from it.

Finally Louise had a hunch and asked, "Did you come from Job's Coffin island?"

"I never hear that name," Manu replied. He pointed off in the direction of the tiny island, however, and said, "I live there."

Louise and Jean dived into the choppy water
to rescue the man

"Then let's go!" Jean urged.

Still Manu did not move. Was he afraid to let them take him there?

Louise was growing exasperated. She decided to make a wild guess. "Manu, you live with Captain Grand, don't you?"

Manu's eyes grew even bigger. "You know him?" he asked. "You know the captain?"

"We are looking for him," Louise said. "We want to tell him about Mr. Platt."

The Danas intently watched Manu's face for a reaction. They were not disappointed. At once he asked fearfully, "Something bad happen to Mr. Platt?"

"He's dead," Jean answered.

Manu closed his eyes as if the shock was too much for him and he almost lost his grasp on the sailboat. Finally he opened his eyes and looked directly at the girls.

"Mr. Platt a good man. He gave Manu this sailboat."

The Danas were jubilant—perhaps the Indian could provide the missing links in the mystery!

Louise now told Manu that Mr. Platt's sister was aboard the seaplane. "Please come with us. I promise we will help you. And you can help us."

Manu at last dropped into the water and began swimming. The Danas followed, and watched him carefully. They saw with relief that he seemed to have enough strength to keep going.

When the three reached the seaplane, eager hands helped Manu aboard. Prof rubbed him briskly with a towel, then threw a raincoat around the shivering Indian.

Louise and Jean told what they had learned from Manu. Everyone was thrilled. Their search for Captain Grand might be almost at an end!

Manu seemed so genuinely grieved over Mr. Platt's death, however, that no one questioned him further. "We'll be on the island soon," Louise murmured to her friends, "and can learn firsthand what the secret of the place is."

Dave took off again and approached their destination. The plane's occupants could see that Job's Coffin was a beautiful little palm tree-covered island with a landlocked harbor. Dave circled twice, then taxied the *Cloud Gull* to the narrow entrance and through two wide-open aluminum gates which reached high above the clear water and down to the sea floor. Suddenly Manu gave a loud cry. All eyes turned on him.

"Captain Grand's boat! It is gone!" the Indian gasped. "And the silver dolphin too!"

CHAPTER XVIII

Carib Legend

AT Manu's announcement, Judy cried out, "What do you mean the silver dolphin is gone?"

The young Indian seemed too overcome to explain. It was not until Dave had moored the seaplane at a small dock and everyone had sat down under a cluster of palm trees that Manu began to talk.

"Over year ago Mr. Platt come here with Captain Grand in his boat. Mr. Platt already own this island."

"Owned it!" Jean broke in, astonished.

"Yes. He visit here but go off for long time. Man from New York in plane bring him and take him away.

"Mr. Platt like dolphins very much. He wanted to catch white one but never did. He say Captain Grand expert, so he hire him full time to look for dolphin and live here."

As Manu paused, Louise asked him, "How did they get food?"

The Indian explained that Captain Grand took his boat to an inhabited island once in a while to pick up supplies. Whenever Mr. Platt came by plane he also brought various things which were needed on the island—tools, machine parts for boat repairs, and clothing.

"My brother must have used this place as his retreat," Judy said. "It *is* peaceful."

"That is what he call it," the Indian youth said. "His retreat."

"Did Captain Grand have any other men with him?" Louise inquired.

Manu nodded. "Two. They live here with him." The Indian continued his story. "One day Mr. Platt and Captain Grand catch silver dolphin. Mr. Platt say it very rare and worth much money. But he would not sell dolphin. He keep it for pet and teach it tricks."

Judy was beaming. "So, my dolphin inheritance is a real, live, silver-colored one," she said. Then she sobered. "Where could Captain Grand have gone, Manu? And why take the dolphin with him? You don't suppose he was going to sell it?"

Manu shook his head violently. "Captain Grand a good man. He not leave this island to do that."

Mr. Erskine spoke up. He felt that the most sensible explanation was that Captain Grand was in need of supplies and had gone off to purchase them.

Afraid to leave the dolphin unguarded, since Manu was away, he had taken the sea mammal along.

The others conceded that this probably was the truth, and once more conversation turned to Judy's inheritance. Prof asked, "Did any of you happen to notice the shape of this island?"

None of them had. Prof said that from the air he had observed that the outline of the island closely resembled that of the constellation Delphinus.

"Judy, you remarked that your brother had once told you he was leaving you two things. Perhaps one of them could have been this very island!"

"That's right," Judy agreed, and added with a chuckle, "It's a strange inheritance, but a pretty nice one. Let's do a little exploring. I'd like to see what my real estate looks like."

Manu was eager to show them around. He seemed to have recovered entirely from his harrowing experience with the overturned sailboat.

"My Carib ancestors live here," he said. "They know island is shape of dolphin. They call it Friendly Sea Beast."

"I like that name much better than Job's Coffin," Anne said.

Manu went on, "The dolphin sacred to ancient people of this island. They make very pretty ones of silver and copper."

Mr. Erskine asked where the ancient Indians had obtained the two metals. Manu surprised the group by saying that they were found right on the island.

"This place top of mountain under sea," the Indian explained. "My ancestors dig down and find silver and copper."

Dave James turned to Judy. "If that's true, you've really inherited some worthwhile property."

Manu said he had come to the island by canoe to dig for treasures his ancestors might have hidden. It was then he had met Mr. Platt, Captain Grand, and the two crewmen. Good-naturedly, they had let Manu stay and dig all he wished to.

"Mr. Platt not seem to believe my story," he said. "But one day he find something himself."

"What was it?" Judy inquired.

"Mr. Platt not tell me that. I think he took it away with him."

"What happened to your ancestors, Manu?" Louise asked. "We were told this was a deserted island."

"It was—after pirates long time ago come here and kill most of my people. A few go away to other islands. Everybody think pirates took treasures from island, but I think some of them still buried."

The Danas and their companions, though intrigued by the story, were tired and hungry. They were all delighted when Manu led them to an attractive palm-thatched cottage Mr. Platt had built. Quickly Manu prepared a light, appetizing meal.

The thought of the missing captain was still uppermost in everyone's mind. "When Captain Grand goes to get supplies, Manu, what time does he usually return?" Jean asked.

"About sunset time. You see island first?"

"Yes."

When everyone had finished eating, Manu led the way around Job's Coffin. He showed them several spots where he had been digging, but admitted he had found nothing.

"Manu not give up," he said determinedly.

Anne, fascinated by the place, ran on ahead of the others. She disappeared from view among the trees and tropical bushes. Suddenly they heard her cry out. Thinking she had come upon something valuable, they rushed forward. But the girl was nowhere in sight.

"Anne! Anne! Where are you?" Mr. Erskine called loudly.

There was no answer. They all exchanged fearful looks. What had happened to Anne? Her father called again and again, but still no response.

"We'll have to make a search," said Louise. "Let's separate, but not lose sight of one another."

"That's a good idea," Prof agreed.

An intensive hunt began. Suddenly Jean pulled

up short. She had almost stepped into a wide hole. Jean knelt and looked down inside the deep, dark excavation. Was it her imagination, or was there a human form lying at the bottom?

No, she was right! The figure began to stir! "Anne!" Jean called. "Anne, is that you?"

The figure did not answer but slowly clawed at the side of the hole, then pulled itself upright.

"Anne!" Jean called again.

A weak voice replied. "Yes. I—I fell in here. It knocked the breath out of me, but I g-guess no bones are broken. I can move all right."

"Thank goodness!" Jean exclaimed. She got to her feet and called loudly to the others, "I've found her! Come here!"

The group quickly gathered. Anne peered up at them ruefully. "How am I ever going to get out?"

Manu said he had dug the hole, searching for artifacts, and felt bad about the accident. He had put steps up one side so that he could climb out. The Indian pointed to them, and Anne slowly pulled herself to the top.

"That was stupid of me," she said. "I should have watched more carefully where I was going."

Manu told her he was very sorry, but Anne insisted he should not blame himself. "I should've let you show me where the danger spots are."

Anne's fall, combined with the fact that the sun

was about to set, sent the group back to the cottage. To their great disappointment, Captain Grand had not returned.

Louise and Jean went off by themselves to talk over the matter. They decided that it would be a good idea for Dave to radio the island where the captain went for supplies.

After some difficulty the pilot managed to contact its airport. His message was relayed to the dock area. After a long wait Dave was told that Captain Grand had not stopped there that day nor the previous one.

The Danas, hearing this, became alarmed. They did not want to worry Judy or Manu, but the two young sleuths feared that Throaty Sensky had come to Job's Coffin with some pals, probably in a chartered plane, during Manu's absence.

"They must have overpowered Captain Grand and his crewmen," Louise said, "and forced him to take them and the silver dolphin away on the *Triton.*"

They confided their suspicions to Dave, who at once radioed on the SOS frequency of 121.5 megacycles to ships and ports. Though the pilot stayed near his shortwave radio for most of the night, no message came in.

None of the party slept well, and by morning everyone was frantic. Judy inadvertently had spoken of their fears in front of Manu, so he too was greatly disturbed.

Jean said, "I suggest we make a search ourselves from the air for Captain Grand's boat."

Mr. Erskine thought they should divide forces. He felt it was not wise to leave the island unguarded. It was the unanimous opinion that Louise and Jean go with Dave in the seaplane.

"We'll hold the fort on land," Anne said with a smile.

After a hasty breakfast the Danas prepared to set off with Dave. Judy was happy to remain behind, saying she wanted to explore "her" dolphin island further.

Manu announced that he had had a dream about a new place to dig for treasure and would be glad to have help. The land group waved to Dave and the sisters as the seaplane took off.

When they were airborne, the pilot told the girls that he must first go to the nearest island where he could refuel. As soon as they reached it, Louise and Jean went ashore also. They questioned various natives for any clue to Captain Grand. But the islanders could tell them nothing. Finally the seaplane was in the air again.

"Have you any suggestions about where to hunt?" Dave asked the girls.

"I have," Louise replied. "If Captain Grand was kidnapped, I believe Throaty would make him head for the mainland."

Dave smiled. "There are thousands of miles of coastline. Which point do you want to try?"

"It's only a guess, but why don't we take the shortest route first?"

Dave agreed and set his course accordingly. An hour later Jean spotted a deep-sea fishing vessel almost directly below them.

"Let's take a look at it," she urged.

Dave swooped toward the boat.

CHAPTER XIX

Runaway Prize

As the seaplane drew near the fishing boat, Dave and the Dana girls cried out in delight at seeing the name on the bow, the *Triton!*

"And look! That big tank built in the deck!" Jean pointed excitedly.

The others gasped. Under the flat canopy which shaded the tank, they glimpsed a beautiful silver dolphin! The netting swept down under it and was draped over the sides of the pool.

"We've found it!" Jean exclaimed. "Judy's silver dolphin!"

"I'm glad the canopy is up," Dave remarked, "because dolphins can get sunburned."

The pilot circled the vessel as Louise grabbed up the binoculars. She trained them on the pilot's canopied section. Suddenly she burst out, "Whoever is running the boat is a prisoner!"

Louise explained that a man wearing an officer's cap was lashed to his chair behind the wheel, with only his arms free to run the ship.

"I'm afraid it's Captain Grand," she said.

Jean and Dave were horrified and asked if anyone else was in sight. Louise said No, but the man was pointing repeatedly to his radio equipment.

"I guess he wants me to contact him," said Dave. "I hope he can pick up the unicom frequency."

The pilot turned on his transmitter and spoke in a low voice so that no one else on board might hear him.

"Calling the *Triton*. *Cloud Gull* calling the *Triton*."

To their relief, the captive answered and said he was Captain Grand, a prisoner of Throaty Sensky, but apparently from fear of being overheard said no more. The Danas assumed his crewmen were prisoners below.

Dave turned to the girls. "What do you think we should do?"

Jean had a prompt reply. "Tell Captain Grand to head back to Job's Coffin."

The pilot was doubtful this would work. "The captain's abductors will certainly catch on," he insisted.

"Maybe not," said Louise. "I have a hunch Throaty and his gang went below when they heard our plane. Down there, they won't know in which direction they're heading."

Dave smiled. "I guess you're right. I'll contact the captain."

Lowering his voice, he radioed the suggestion, telling the captain that friends were awaiting him on Oliver Platt's island in case of any trouble. Within seconds, the *Triton* began to turn, making a slow, deliberate arc.

"It's going to work!" Jean cried out jubilantly.

The boat had barely straightened out when a man poked his head up from a companionway.

"He must be one of Throaty's men!" Louise exclaimed.

The words were hardly out of her mouth when a loud, sharp-tongued command was heard over Dave's radio. "Warn that plane to leave us alone, Grand," yelled a hoarse voice, "or I'll fire on it!"

"That's Throaty!" Jean exclaimed.

Dave looked worried. He immediately took the seaplane into a steep climb. "I don't want to take a chance with you girls aboard," he said.

"But we aren't just going to let that thief win, are we?" Louise asked.

Dave agreed to keep flying in the area to be sure the *Triton* kept bearing toward the island. But he flew at an altitude too high for fire from a long-range rifle to reach.

To the girls' delight, the dolphin ship kept heading directly for Friendly Sea Beast Island. Presently the boat began to move faster.

"I wonder if Captain Grand decided to increase

speed, or did Throaty?" Dave asked the girls.

The young sleuths felt that Throaty had given the order. Louise said, "He must still believe they're heading for the mainland, and wants to get there as quickly as possible and escape before a report reaches the police."

Suddenly Captain Grand's voice came over the radio in a whisper. "I'll sign off so you can call for help."

Dave tried hard to reach some nearby station or operator who might happen to be tuned into the SOS signal. He could not raise anyone. Finally he gave up.

"I guess we'll have to handle this ourselves," Dave concluded. "We'd better go back to the island pronto and alert the others."

They were within sight of the dolphin-shaped island now. In a short time they landed and taxied through the opening to the harbor. For the first time, Louise noticed that the gates, which operated manually, were of the swinging type, with each half hinged to a stout post on either side of the entrance. Dave assumed that the gates had been put there to keep the silver dolphin from escaping while he was frolicking in the harbor.

The plane glided up to the dock. Everyone was there to greet them, eager to find out what they had learned. Quickly the story was told.

"You saw the silver dolphin!" Judy cried out. "Oh, how marvelous!"

"Yes, and he's absolutely beautiful!" Jean exclaimed.

Mr. Erskine at once began to give orders on preparing to do battle with Throaty Sensky and any pals he had with him. He suggested that Dave stay in the seaplane outside the harbor entrance.

"Keep the engine running in case you have to take off in a hurry to summon help."

Prof and Manu were to stay on the dock to be ready to board the *Triton* as soon as possible.

"What about us girls?" Anne asked. "We can help too."

Her father shook his head. "I can't permit any of you to risk getting hurt. You'd better go up to the cottage."

The four girls looked glum. They had worked so hard to solve the mystery! The Danas especially felt left out of what they knew would be a dramatic encounter.

Suddenly Jean had an idea. "Mr. Erskine," she said, "we couldn't possibly get hurt if we stayed underwater."

Mr. Erskine looked at her in surprise. "What's clicking in that head of yours, young lady?" he asked.

"I was just thinking," Jean replied, "that we girls might put on our swim suits, take the scuba gear we brought, and wait near the harbor entrance. Then we'll be out of the way of any fight. But we'll be able to see what's going on."

Mr. Erskine smiled. "That seems fair enough," he conceded. "But you'd better hurry."

The girls rushed up to the cottage, changed into their swim suits, and grabbed the scuba equipment. Then they dashed back to the dock and adjusted their diving equipment. Just ahead, outside the harbor, they could see the *Triton* making ready to enter.

Quickly the four girls let themselves into the water and swam to the entrance. They took positions where, undetected, they could watch the boat come in.

Two men stood on deck. One, dark-haired and of medium height, was at the fore end of the tank. The girls felt sure he was Throaty. His assistant was at the stern. Throaty held up his hands as if in surrender.

He yelled, "We'll give up if you'll promise not to fight!"

"All right," Mr. Erskine called back from the dock, "but no tricks!"

The Danas could see a look of cunning come over Throaty's face. He shouted back, "You'll never enjoy the prize you came to get!"

The girls wondered what he meant. They did not have long to find out. Throaty and his buddy lifted up the canopy over the pool, then cranked up the net that held the silver dolphin and swung it to the side of the *Triton*. In a second they loosened it.

The dolphin and net went overboard and disappeared beneath the water with a tremendous splash!

"Oh!" cried Judy. "He'll get away!"

"We'll try to capture him!" said Louise. "Maybe he can't get out of the net!"

By the time the girls had gone underwater, the silver dolphin had extricated itself from the net and was speeding toward the open sea!

The Danas knew they could not hope to catch it. But knowing the dolphin was a pet, they hoped it might circle around and somehow they could entice it back into the harbor. Then they would close the gates.

To make better speed, the girls rose to the surface. In the meantime, Throaty had spotted them. Furious that he might have been outwitted, he dived overboard and raced after the four swimmers. The discarded net was floating on the water. Throaty grabbed it in one hand and swam along.

Louise, Jean, and Anne were delighted to see that the dolphin had suddenly surfaced, and with arcing leaps and dives, was heading back toward them.

At that moment Louise realized that Judy was not with them. She looked back and noticed the red-haired girl was lagging far behind.

"Poor Judy! The strain has been too much for her," Louise thought, "and she's lost her energy."

Louise went back to help her friend. But before

she could reach her, Louise saw with horror that Throaty, dragging the huge net in one hand, was closing in on Judy.

Suddenly panic seized Louise. She was sure the thief was planning to drown Judy for spite!

"I must save her!" Louise put on a burst of speed, swam up to the weary girl, and tried to pull her out of the way.

But she was not in time. Throaty had overtaken them. He flung the net and the next moment the two girls were hopelessly enmeshed in it!

CHAPTER XX

Detective Sea Creature

THROATY SENSKY left the two girls struggling inside the net and made a dash for the seaplane. Meanwhile, Captain Grand had brought the *Triton* to the dock. Quickly Mr. Erskine, Prof, and Manu climbed aboard. Mr. Erskine cut the ropes which bound Captain Grand. Manu and Prof freed his two crewmen and brought them on deck, together with Throaty's pals.

Suddenly they were amazed to see Throaty starting to climb aboard the seaplane. The next moment his fist lashed out as he tried to land a punch on Dave's jaw. The pilot dodged. Like a shot he was out of his plane and grappling with the thief in the water.

The battle was over in fifteen seconds as Dave gave Throaty a stiff uppercut and the thief flopped back into the water. He was helped aboard the

Triton. Though completely cowed, he wore a sardonic sneer on his face but said nothing.

"What did you hope to accomplish by knocking me out?" Dave asked him.

"I was going to take your plane and get away. What else?"

"And leave your pals behind?" Dave said in disgust. Throaty did not reply.

Throaty's captors did not ask him any more questions because by this time they were thoroughly alarmed about the whereabouts of the four girls. Had they gone a long distance after the dolphin and perhaps been carried out to sea—and swept away?

At that very moment Louise and Judy were in great danger, struggling desperately to get free of the net Throaty had thrown over them. But the more they struggled, the more tightly enmeshed they became.

Louise fought down a fresh wave of panic. "We have to keep calm!" she thought.

Just when their plight seemed hopeless, the silver dolphin suddenly turned around and came toward them. He apparently sensed that the girls were in trouble, perhaps because he knew that net all too well! With his strong dorsal fin he ripped great gashes in the net.

"Oh, you blessed creature!" Louise said. She clung to the mammal's flipper and patted his hard rubbery side.

A wave of affection for the dolphin swept over Judy too. She stroked him, then grabbed hold of his dorsal fin. He seemed to know that she wanted to be taken ashore and made no protest. Louise dropped back as the big mammal sped away.

Despite the weight he was pulling, the dolphin made marvelous time back to the harbor.

Jean and Anne had seen the rescue and turned back to give Louise their help if she needed it. The three girls followed Judy and the dolphin. When they reached the gates, Jean and Anne closed them so that Judy's prize could not get away again.

"Thank goodness you're back," said Dave as the girls swam to the dock.

Judy told what had happened and everyone glared at Throaty, who was now their prisoner. As the swimmers dried off in the sun and the dolphin frisked about in the water, a full confession was obtained from the thief.

He admitted to being in the employ of Maria Castone, who, he said, was a very clever woman and had a considerable amount of money stowed away. She had engineered all the moves Throaty had made, with the exception of kidnapping the silver dolphin.

"That was my own idea," he said proudly. Throaty went on, "Maria wanted to get that reward money, and when she makes up her mind to something, there's no stopping her."

The others learned that Throaty and his two pals

had come to Job's Coffin island on a chartered plane the day before the Danas had arrived. They had made a surprise attack on Captain Grand and his two men, while Manu had been away in the sailboat.

Captain Grand added, "Throaty had us at a disadvantage and we were forced to put the silver dolphin aboard and head for the mainland. If you and the seaplane hadn't come along and swooped down low enough to see us, we might have had to go all the way."

He glared angrily at the thief. "A kidnapping charge is a very serious offense," he reminded Throaty and his pals.

Throaty admitted to having had a boy deliver the box with the note and the scorpions to Judy's apartment.

"Maria knew about the stars Mr. Platt used around his signature, because once he scribbled them on a piece of paper while he was at her studio."

Looking directly at the thief, Judy asked him, "Where is the rest of my Master Mining stock?"

After a minute's silence Throaty growled, "I didn't sell much of the stock I brought with me. Most of it's in Miami."

The Danas told Captain Grand about the stolen securities, then Jean queried the prisoner. "Why did you give one share of stock to Wally Wallace?"

Throaty scowled. "That was a mistake. I meant to pull a different paper from my pocket that didn't mean anything."

Louise asked him, "Did you hide the stock under the cushion of the rocking chair at your friend Bengler's house?"

Throaty admitted that he had. "It was my own idea, and I must say you were smart to find it. My friend is innocent."

"It's your fault he's in jail," Jean put in.

Throaty actually looked sad at this reminder. He shouted in his hoarse voice, "He's not in our racket. They got to let him go!"

Mr. Erskine said that as soon as they could relay a message to the mainland he would be in touch with the police and Bengler would be freed.

Jean remarked, "You were the person who threw the bundle of newspapers at my uncle, weren't you?"

"Yes, I was," the prisoner admitted. "Maria thought if I did that it would frighten your aunt and uncle and they wouldn't let you work on the mystery."

Throaty said that it was also Maria's idea that he break into the Dana home and try to find out the girls' plans. He had heard Miss Dana and the maid talking about Miami where the girls were going.

"I thought," Throaty added, "that I would find their address in the bags, but it wasn't in them. So I searched all the drawers. I hadn't quite finished when your aunt came in and I had to get out the window in a hurry."

Throaty said he had nothing more to admit than that he had hired the boy on the beach to throw the stone. He lay down on the dock and closed his eyes, completely exhausted.

Conversation among the others turned toward Captain Grand and his stay at the island. He said Mr. Platt, who ordinarily used a chartered plane from New York, had paid him well for coming and remaining there.

"After we caught the silver dolphin, Mr. Platt wanted it guarded day and night. At first he thought of selling it to some aquarium, but he became so fond of the sea mammal that he could not part with it. Let me show you one of its tricks."

Captain Grand walked off a little way and from behind a tree brought a long pole with a large hoop at the end. He walked to the dock and whistled. Instantly the dolphin's head came up. The captain held out the pole and said, "Ready, Star! Get set! Jump!"

The dolphin rose high in the air and went through the hoop without touching it. The audience clapped enthusiastically. At the sound, the dolphin surfaced and squealed.

"Oh, I'm never going to sell Star!" Judy exclaimed. "I'll talk to Mr. Howell and have him help me figure out what I can do with this island and my beautiful new pet."

Dave grinned. "This would make a wonderful tourist attraction. Maybe I could bring sightseers over here in my seaplane."

Judy laughed. "It sounds good. Let's talk it over later."

"Later is right," said Dave. "I must try getting a message through so your prisoners can be turned over to the authorities." He got back into the seaplane and worked at his radio for a long time.

Finally he succeeded in having a message relayed until it reached the Miami police. He also asked that the Oak Falls police be alerted to arrest Maria Castone, and finally, that Mrs. Erskine, Captain Dana and his sister and Mr. Howell be notified. At Judy's request, the trust officer was invited to come down to the island to view her inheritance personally.

"And of course you'll receive the reward. You really deserve it." Judy smiled at the Danas.

"Thanks," said Louise. "But our best reward is finding the dolphin."

Both she and Jean sighed wistfully, thinking, "This is the end of the mystery. When will another come along?" One soon did—THE MYSTERY OF THE WAX QUEEN.

As the pilot signed off, the silver dolphin began to shake its head and squeal insistently. The girls laughed and Jean asked, "What's on your mind, Star?"

The sea creature dived, came up again, squealed, then dived once more.

"I believe it wants to show us something underwater," Louise guessed.

The four girls and Manu put on their scuba gear and dived in. They followed the dolphin as it swam to the opposite side of the harbor, then went down thirty feet to the sea floor.

"Star's taking us to a cave!" the girls thought.

To their amazement, the dolphin suddenly stopped and poked its snout against something. In the dim light the girls could not see what it was, but they felt the shape of the object.

"This must be a chest!" Louise decided.

She tugged at it and finally with the help of Manu brought the chest to the surface. They swam to the dock, as the others followed.

"My word, what's in it?" Mr. Erskine asked in amazement as everyone helped to open the chest.

Inside lay several ancient artifacts of silver and copper!

Manu stared in disbelief. "Good things my ancestors make!" he exclaimed. The Indian tenderly lifted out one after another of the objects.

"Your Carib ancestors must have hidden these from the pirates," Anne remarked.

Louise said she doubted this. "If they had, the treasure chest would have been buried more deeply by this time."

"Then who put it there?" Judy asked.

Louise smiled. "Your brother, I believe. He found the artifacts on the island and put them in the chest. If you take a close look, you'll see that the chest is not very old."

Suddenly the silver dolphin began to squeal again. Everyone looked at him and laughed while he bobbed his head back and forth as if saying, "Yes, you're right." Judy beamed at her new possession.

Jean remarked with a wink, "Judy, the dolphin probably saw your brother hide the chest. That's how Star knew enough to tell you, as the new owner of Friendly Sea Beast Island, where it was!"